John M. Fothergill

Gaythorne Hall

Vol. II

John M. Fothergill

Gaythorne Hall
Vol. II

ISBN/EAN: 9783337066239

Printed in Europe, USA, Canada, Australia, Japan

Cover: Foto ©Andreas Hilbeck / pixelio.de

More available books at **www.hansebooks.com**

GAYTHORNE HALL

A Novel

BY

JOHN M. FOTHERGILL

' 'Tis greatly wise to talk with our past hours,
And ask them what report they bore to heaven,
And how they might have borne more welcome news.'
YOUNG.

IN THREE VOLUMES.

VOL. II.

LONDON:
HURST AND BLACKETT, PUBLISHERS,
13, GREAT MARLBOROUGH STREET,
1884.

CONTENTS OF VOL. II.

GAYTHORNE HALL.

CHAPTER I.

IN GAYTHORNE HALL.

His failure to discover the murderer of
Tom Earnshaw, and his firm conviction
that the dastardly deed was perpetrated by
some of the dangerous elements of society,
known then as 'physical force' Chartists,
embittered Squire Wharton against the
movement in its entirety. He was opposed
to it by nature. A patrician by descent, his
sympathies were with the few; and not with
the many. He honestly believed in his
heart that the people would be much better
off and happier under rulers selected for
them by existing social arrangements, than

if legislated for by their own representatives. He looked upon this general craving for a voice in the making of the laws by which they were governed, pretty much as a schoolmaster would regard a demand on the part of his scholars to have some say in the regulations by which he ruled them : a sort of boyish craze for something they had no business with. The people ought to do as they were told ! It was a simple arrangement ; much better for them, if they only would believe it, than anything they could possibly devise for themselves. Then, again, as an old soldier he hated turbulence ; and the union of the violent ' physical force ' Chartists,—all the dissatisfied idlers and ruffians who hated the new Poor Law, the ' chargeable labourers ' of the old Poor Law, to the ' moral force ' Chartists, only served to damn the others in his eyes. That, as Jim Woodcock reminded him, they had no love for this addition to their ranks as reformers, weighed little with him by the side of the fact, that the Charter movement had contrived to attract to it, and so to give some cohesion to them, the scattered elements of dissatisfaction over the country. He lived near Sheffield and Barnsley on the one hand ; and not very far from Manchester and the eastern fringe of the cotton-districts on the other. Over the moors, which lay between these and Hallamshire (as this area of Yorkshire is often termed), the wilder spirits of each area could pass by night ; and so find shelter when wanted by the police for some deed of violence. It was easy when necessary to cross the moors under the shelter of night, and all trace of their existence was lost. This facility encouraged the class who profited by the natural advantages for concealment offered by these circumstances ; and that class was a large one. This the Squire well knew, as an owner of pheasant-preserves. The idle fellow, or the lawless ruffian, is always a poacher at heart. To drink at low public-houses in the day, and then to poach at night has an attraction for a certain section of the proletariat

which seems all too powerful for their capa-
cities for self-restraint. Where there are a
number of resident gentry all of whom are
game preservers, in the neighbourhood of
towns where violence is common and little
condemned by the local opinion, a feud is
sure to exist;—born of mutual injury, of
punishment for offences, and revenge induced thereby. Sheffield always had an
evil reputation for deeds of violence, which
seemed to excite comparatively little public
indignation. Tom Earnshaw was a faithful
gamekeeper, who not only resented the
spoiling of his master's preserves; but had
an instinctive dislike of the class who
furnished poachers, and of the lawless, useless lives they led. That he had fallen a
victim to the revenge of some one whom he
had been instrumental in bringing to punishment, was the generally accepted belief of
the whole country-side.

With the Squire the conviction was so
strong that Tom had been sacrificed to the
revenge of some of these ' physical force '

men, and was but an instance of what they were prepared to do, that his antagonism to the whole Chartist movement was intensified. The torchlight meetings and processions which formed a part of the demonstrations of the Chartist rabble of the towns, were common in Sheffield and the towns lying near to it. Many of the younger fellows carried pikes; and some no doubt brandished firearms, which weapons could not be exhibited in daylight. The terror caused by the exaggerated alarms which were propagated on every side, about these torchlight gatherings, was intense. All respectable timid people were nearly beside themselves with fear. This terror greatly gratified the youngsters who formed the great bulk of these gatherings, and processions; and encouraged them to continue their practices. Calmer and more judicious persons saw that these foolish meetings greatly added to the alarm, that really had valid grounds for its existence; and that consequently it was well to put a check upon them. In the middle of December, 1838, these torchlight demonstrations were forbidden. Squire Wharton had felt all a magistrate's dislike to such demonstrations; and, as an old soldier, held them in the utmost contempt as factors in putting any pressure on the Government.

'A pack of silly lads,' he said one day to his housekeeper, as she arranged the cushion for his gouty foot; an attack of gout having fastened on him; 'led by men who are old enough to know better; but who don't! What do they expect to come of it? Nobody is frightened—well, nobody ought to be frightened. I am sure none of mine are, at least. Are you frightened, Mrs. Allonby?' he would ask.

'Well, no, sir, not frightened; but of course, sir, I don't approve of them. I often say to Mary—"We needn't be afraid; master only laughs at them." But when we hear the tales that come into the servants' hall, we don't like the idea of being out after dark.'

'And a very good thing for Mary, too; going out after dark is a very imprudent practice for a good-looking girl like her. So far as she is concerned, she may be thankful for the Chartists.'

'Mary's a steady girl, sir,' replied Mrs. Allonby, jealous for her niece's reputation; 'she does not go tramping out at nights like the girls at Satanstoe; who won't leave the young fellows alone, if the men would let them alone.'

'That's your opinion, Mrs. Allonby, about the relation of the sexes at Satanstoe, is it?' Mrs. Allonby was puzzled with the phraseology employed—'the relation of the sexes' sounded foreign to her ears. So she went back to the original topic.

'There are wild stories about as to what's being done. It's said that down at Satanstoe some of the colliers have been getting pikes ready; and one has been seen casting bullets, it's reported. It's like some of us are frightened.'

'Casting bullets; has he indeed? He

would be wise to throw them away when he
has cast them. Bullets indeed! I suppose
he thinks people will be scared by bullets.
Well they may if they know little about
them. But if the 32nd were only here
now, they would soon let them see how
little they care about bullets. But they are
in Canada. Never mind: there are plenty
as good in England.'

'But the Chartists say, sir, the soldiers
are with them. That when the time comes
the soldiers will side with them.'

'Then they tell a —— lie, Mrs. Allonby,
whoever says so. It's a false calumny! A
British soldier obeys his officers. He knows
that the officers understand what they are
doing: and he obeys orders. Don't tell
me any such nonsense!'

Mrs. Allonby went in great respect of the
Squire, and even the familiarity which
must necessarily obtain under such circumstances as existed at Gaythorne Hall, never
materially lessened it. The Squire was not
given to swearing; as a Wharton, he rather

looked down upon it;—however prevalent the custom of profane swearing might still be among squires. Whenever he did swear it was always to give emphasis to what he was saying, and it was not his custom to be thus emphatic. Consequently, when he did swear, Mrs. Allonby perfectly comprehended the significance of the act. The charge of disloyalty in the troops fired the old soldier in the Squire.

'I'm sure I'm glad to hear it, sir. But there is a many who say that if it is not true, it is very likely all the same. The soldiers are working folks themselves; and they hold their own opinions.'

'Stuff and rubbish, I tell you!' This was still more emphatic, for Squire Wharton was accustomed to treat his housekeeper with respect. He did not wish to disparage her opinions; he merely wished to assuage her alarms. He felt such alarm was unbecoming in the household of an ex-officer magistrate.

'Now, Mrs. Allonby, there is no need to be afraid at all. Don't believe half the stories you hear; and only half of those that you do believe. It's part of their plan to set these stories about. But they shall not say that they are believed at Gaythorne Hall. So I beg of you put them aside as idle talk. Discourage such tales as much as you can, Mrs. Allonby. Make them understand I give no credence to these stories. They won't frighten me into yielding anything to fear.'

'But then you see, sir, we can't forget about poor Tom Earnshaw. It is only a week or two since he was found murdered.'

'To be sure; to be sure. Of course you naturally cannot forget that. Poor Tom! The reward has brought out nothing. I suppose his end will be held up as a warning. Poor honest fellow! They would not have scared him with all their bluster. Tom would just have kept his eye on them And they knew it; and that's why they shot him, the cowardly assassins! My blood boils to think of that dastardly deed! Who is supposed to have done it, Mrs. Allonby?

What does report say ?   Has Bulman heard anything ?'

'The tale that is going is that it was the work of some Sheffield fellows; who bore him a grudge.'

'Sheffield men bore him a grudge ! How is that ?'

'Well, a year or two since, there were some Sheffield men transported for poaching on the Stanhope estates ; and Tom, if you remember, sir, said that he saw some of these very Sheffield men out in this direction that evening ; and this upset the alibi they were setting up, that they were at home that night. The Stanhope keepers might have been mistaken in the dark. And they say it was Tom's evidence that got the men transported.

'Oh yes. I remember about it. A good many threats were made at the time about what they would do. Tom told me what they said, laughing, and saying they would have to catch him asleep before they could do what they threatened. And they have watched him all this time ?'

'Yes.   It seems that is what Dan Appleyard believes.   He swears it was never
done by any Satanstoe men.'

'Well, he is like to know about it if it
was done by Satanstoe men.   I am glad it
was not any of them.   But they are not
above suspicion.   I wish we could find out
who did it.'

'Tunstall says it makes him afraid sometimes when he is out at night, when he
thinks about poor Tom.'

'Well, if they have any grudge at him,
I think the men that did for Tom will soon
dispose of Tunstall.'

'I'm sure I hope not, sir.   You don't
think there is any fear of it, do you, sir?'

'None at all.   No more does Tunstall.
He's a plucky fellow enough.   I merely
meant that if they could do for Tom Earnshaw,—who was a wide-awake fellow, they
would have no difficulty with Tunstall if
they were so minded.   But he is safe
enough '

Here the conversation was interrupted

by a loud knocking at the front door. Mrs.
Allonby took her departure at once without
a hint. The old Squire often had a talk
with his trusty housekeeper; but he had no
mind to have the fact generally known.

Gaythorne Hall was a pleasant place
when looked at from a distance. It was
situated on the slope of the rising ground
running up from the rich alluvial plain
of the Don to the moors above Brigstone.
The slope faced eastwards, and caught the
rising sun; and consequently turned its back
upon the west, so that in the winter evenings it was cold and sombre. But the many
fires took away from any feeling of chilli-
ness which might thus be engendered.
Within it was cosy and comfortable.

The house itself was a rather plain struc-
ture, dating back to the Stuarts. There
was nothing mediæval about it; no Eliza-
bethan battlements which might be utilized
for defence in case of attack. It was too
far away from the Scottish border to require
embattlements; nor was there any moat

or other military work around it. It was
a solid, two-story building, with attics and
dormer windows, standing out from its red-
tiled roof. It faced south-east, and looked
down the rich slope where the tall chimneys
of Wybrow might on a clear day be seen
in the distance. It was a substantial building, if perfectly plain. It was almost entirely covered with green foliage : there was
ivy in abundance, a magnolia, some Gloire
de Dijon roses, some pink monthly roses,
and at the south-eastern corner variegated
ivy, whose leaves set off the other foliage
to advantage. Away into the slope of the
hill stretched the domestic portion of the
building—the offices and the stables. In
front was an extensive lawn, with flower-
beds and evergreens. One of its main
features was its rosary, which had a great
local reputation. The locality was rather
high for the fragrant shrub; but watchful
attention had protected the trees, so that
the winter frosts had little effect upon them.
It was surrounded by a belt of evergreens

to break the blasts. As soon as the leaves began to fall the standards were swathed in straw, and some refuse from the stables piled around the stem so as to keep the roots warm. When spring came the winter envelopes were removed, the ground gently stirred over the roots, and the rosary put on its summer aspect. Consequently this rosary flourished, and every one liked to take a stroll through it with its scented perfume, and its lovely and varied roses. Despite the altitude, a monkey-puzzle was to be seen here and there. An acacia struggled up at intervals; and, strange to say, at one point of the drive was a southerly product,—a sumach itself. The drive, running out into the main road, went through a dense row of lime-trees, which gave a grateful shade in summer; and also made the drive intensely dark on cloudy nights.

Within, Gaythorne Hall was as plain and substantial as was its exterior. To the northern edge of its front stood the dining-room, and behind that a library or study, whose few old-fashioned vellum-bound volumes looked as if they were rarely disturbed,—which constituted the Squire's favourite sitting-room. Both these rooms were dark and sombre, from the oak panels which covered the walls. The use of oak panels by Cardinal Wolsey at Hampton Court Palace had led to their extensive use; and Gaythorne Hall shared in the fashion. The oak was darkened by time and the smoke from the fire, which had often been laid with peat from the moors; and peat-smoke it is which gives the rich hue to old oak furniture. But the peat-smoke was a thing of the past. The Satanstoe collieries had put an end to peat-fires. But the dark oak panels told their own story; and further testified to the bees'-wax and turpentine and the elbow-polish which had been unsparingly lavished upon them. In the ruddy glow of the firelight, and the moderated flame of the lamp, the study looked both picturesque and comfortable; while the polished dark surfaces of the panels in the dining-room reflected the silver, of which Gaythorne Hall had an ample share. Silver dishes looked well against the dark background; and when lighted up for dinner, with a good log on the fire, so as not to give out much heat, and the massive silver candlesticks, the room looked striking, and even imposing. Over that solid dining-table the Whartons of the past had drank the health of the exiled Stuarts. 'Here's to the King!' (over the water—indicated by passing the wine-glass, or goblet over any water-jug near at hand) was drank as a religious ceremony. Gatherings had been held here when the Scotch upheld the claims of the Stuarts in arms; but these Whartons escaped the fate which overtook the main branch of the family. When claret became scarce in the struggle with Napoleon, the port of Portugal came into vogue; and the Squire's father had laid in a great stock, which Squire Charles had heavily mulcted. The room looked like solid comfort; and the impression so made tallied with the facts.

The drawing-room occupied the southern aspect of the front, and was a bright, airy room; partly from the amount of sunlight which found its way into it from its position, partly from the style in which it was furnished. Its furniture consisted of sofa and chairs, the latter of the spindle-legged pattern, of rosewood upholstered in blue satin damask. There were also several occasional chairs, elaborately carved with spiral legs, which were covered with handsome needle or bead-work, the execution of the late Mrs. Wharton. There were also other evidences of that lady's skill with her needle in the form of footstools, cushions, and a fire-screen—a group of tiger-lilies worked in chenille on canvas — a very clever piece of work. The windows were hung with handsome blue satin damask curtains, headed with a solid gilded cornice. There were only one or two ornaments upon the mantel-piece, but they were in harmony with the rest of the room. Over the mantel-piece rose a tall mirror. In one window stood a buhl-and-marqueterie table; while opposite the windows stood a Chippendale cabinet filled with Indian work, and other curiosities the Squire had brought from Canada.

This room was the object of the most solicitous care on the part of Mrs. Allonby, though it was rarely used; as the Squire disliked it, and never entered it when he could avoid doing so. When lady-visitors called they were shown into it with much ceremony, as if they ought to be as much impressed with it as were the occupants of Gaythorne Hall; the Squire alone excepted.

But such visitors were few. Ceremonial calls had scarcely found their way into the hills, and the people who visited Squire Wharton came to see him because they wished to see him; not to leave a card devoutly hoping that he was not at home. His niece always shunned the room, and

made her way into the study without ado;
except when she had argued with herself as
she came up the drive that she really must
see the drawing-room, else Mrs. Allonby
would be so disappointed. After such
resolve she would, with a sense of duty,
look into the forsaken room, and compli-
ment Mrs. Allonby upon the attention paid
to it; which was but an act of justice.
Miss Oldfield always took scrupulous care
to carefully inspect the room and give her
share of admiration to it, and the care be-
stowed upon it. Other ladies knew the old
housekeeper's foibles, and remembered to
gratify her.

Behind these front rooms were a multi-
plicity of other rooms. Immediately behind
the drawing-room was a cosy little room
looking south. This had been a sort of
boudoir in old Mrs. Wharton's day; but
Squire Charles gave it up to the old housekeeper, and when Mrs. Allonby succeeded
to her, the room became hers. Here she
spent a good deal of her spare time; knit-

ting vigorously, and bestowing much good advice, and affording much instruction to her niece, Mary Jessop, a good-looking girl, with a round face, dark eyes, black wavy hair, and a high-coloured complexion. Mary had been adopted by her aunt, and, it was understood, had to inherit all her savings; that is, provided she married according to her aunt's wishes. Such prospects, in addition to her good looks and her steady conduct, made Mary the object of many attentions on the part of the young men of the neighbourhood; though she was still but very young.

The next most important personage at Gaythorne Hall was Bulman, the Squire's valet. If he had a Christian name it was unknown. Had Bulman been able to write, no doubt some indication of the existence of a Christian name would have been furnished by his signature occasionally; but Bulman's accomplishments were not of a literary character. He could read freely enough when he had print to deal with;

and he could make out the address of a
letter—especially the Squire's, by the J.P.
after the name—though not always successfully; but there his powers ended. He had
been the Squire's servant in Canada while
a private in his regiment; and a more
devoted servant never existed. His fidelity
induced the Squire to take him with him to
England on his return; and as his friends
lived far away in Devonshire, Bulman never
went to see them, but kept resolutely to
Gaythorne Hall. The Squire had become
so thoroughly habituated to Bulman's at-
tendance that it had become a matter of
course to him; and what he would have
done without Bulman was as little a matter
of conjecture with him as was that of the
presence of the sun itself.

Bulman was rarely ill. His habits were
active; for hours in the day he was left to
himself, but when the dinner-hour drew
nigh, he reappeared with mathematical
certainty. He was a middle-sized, firmly-
built man, who kept up his soldierly bear-

ing; and 'the Squire's man,' as he was designated, was a well-known figure in Brigstone. All the gentry around had a word for him, for all respected him; and though he did stand behind their chair at dinner, that matter did not affect them materially. A first-rate waiter he was too; as all knew.

It was held among the gossips of Brigstone that Bulman and Mrs. Allonby would make a match of it, despite their disparity in years, (for she was nearly ten years his senior,) if anything happened to the Squire; but for such speculation there was no warrant. Bulman quickly took in the position of Mrs. Allonby when he came to Gaythorne Hall; and, comprehending it, never forgot it. Consequently they got on well together, each respecting the other; and the subordinate domestics recognized their respective positions; and as much domestic peace obtained at Gaythorne Hall in its internal arrangements as was compatible with human nature and its susceptibilities.

Of the latter there was an abundance; some thrifty managers might have thought a super-abundance; but they contrived to keep out of each other's way, and consequently no excess was felt as a matter of experience. All looked up to the Squire with a respect which almost amounted to awe. He was ever kind and thoughtful; but when it became necessary to be stern he acted like the ex-soldier he was. Bulman had a tale or two to tell of prompt action in Canada which added to this impression.

There was a genial sense of ease and plenty in the Hall which was to become a contrast to the want surging around it, as the winter went on; and the pinch of dear food was telling on the working-classes. Some of the famishing Chartists of the riotous order used to talk of firing the place some night; but they scarcely meant it; it was a vague threat, the outcome of the plenty of the servants' hall, and of the contrast of their ill-furnished larders. Bulman smiled contemptuously when the threats reached his ears. ' It is easier said than done, they'll find,' was all he said. One peculiarity there was about Bulman, and that was, his speech was entirely free from any northern accent. The women of the place always said, ' Bulman speaks loike the gentle folks thersens.'

When the Squire's birthday came round it was kept in good old-fashioned style in the servants' hall. There was plenty of beef and ale, and when Bulman gave ' the Squire's health,' the response, ' With all my

heart,' rang out musically, and with genuine feeling. Then ' Mr. John and Miss Edith,' followed, and again rang out ' With all my heart.' After that they sang ' A fine old English gentleman,' in good old-fashioned style; the doors being left open for the Squire to hear the mirth. But all was within reason; and the festivity

never degenerated into revelry. Bulman
took care of that.

From all of which it will be seen that
the housekeeping at Gaythorne Hall was
conducted on the liberal scale which had
always obtained there. All were happy
and comfortable, or were so as far as that
could be done by kindly thoughtfulness ;
and there was not one of the numerous
household who would not have gone great
lengths in the way of devotion to their
master, whom they loved and revered.

CHAPTER II.

THE FIRST JAR.

THE front door opened at the summons of the knocker, and Bulman let in Mr. John Wharton; who, after asking kindly how all of them were, turned from the entrance-hall into his uncle's study.

'Glad to see thee, Jack,' was the Squire's hearty greeting.

'Thank you, uncle; how are you? Only pretty well, I fear. Your old enemy has been paying you a visit!'

'That he has. Nothing brings on the gout with me so certainly as any trouble. That affair of Earnshaw's has upset me terribly. I feel I am getting an old man!'

'Don't say that, uncle. You're only a

little over sixty. I am sure I wish you may live other twenty years.'

'Thank you, Jack. I know you mean it. And it's not every man in our positions who could say such a thing,—and find the other believe it; but I do, I assure you. Only I don't want to linger on an old doting hulk to watch you growing old,—waiting for what must be yours. I don't want that!'

'You are always most generous, uncle; but don't let us talk of the time when you shall have passed away from Gaythorne Hall. Is the gout any better?'

'A trifle. Mr. Roebuck says he thinks I shall have a longish turn of it this time. And, faith! I think he will turn out to be right.'

'I don't suppose he will fret much about that; as long as he comes to see you. Don't you think it might be well to see some one else as well? To get Grinder from Sheffield to meet him here?'

'Not if I keep my faculties, Jack! One

doctor can give me medicine quite nasty enough; I don't know what two would do; and I'd rather not think of it. The gout and one doctor, Jack, you will find are quite enough at once; when you come to try the experiment.'

'It is an experiment I have no wish to try, I can assure you. If ever I get the gout, it will not be from any fault of my own.'

'I believe you. If gluttony and wine-bibbing bring gout, as is said.'

'I don't think you got it that way, uncle.'

'Well, perhaps not; but I have taken no great pains to avoid it. You may stick to claret, Jack. But 1820 port has a charm about it. I am afraid I shall have to get through what there is of it, else it will be wasted; and that will mean a good deal of gout.' The old Squire was no hard drinker, but he loved his port; and surveyed his gouty foot with that sweet consciousness of guilt which has been a source of much comfort to many persons when they were reaping as they had sowed. 'I suppose it is very shocking to talk so, but I am not very afraid of the gout.'

'If you were, it would be the only thing you are afraid of, uncle.'

'No, Jack, there is one thing I always have been afraid of,—and I hope always will be afraid of, Jack.'

'Whatever is that, uncle?'

'Afraid of not doing my duty, my boy.'

'That's it! I could not think what it was.'

'I hope no Wharton will ever be afraid of anything but that. They may act wrongly, but it must be from bad judgment: never from a bad motive. We may be unwise at times, but never wicked. That is the character of the Whartons.'

'Do you think it held quite good of the famous election-carrying Wharton? There are some rather doubtful actions in his life, I fear.'

' There were some things hard to excuse by our lights. He lived in an age for which great allowances must be made. Charles II. set a bad example; and a bad example is easily copied. We must take that into consideration. He was a remarkable man, though.'

' I think the character of the Whartons of the past has been such that we can look back without qualms. I hope we shall not degenerate.' Jack stopped suddenly, arrested by the consciousness of the fact that his Chartist leanings were an offence to his uncle; who regarded him as having fallen from his natural height in adopting views so unpalatable to patricians; and who grieved over him as a sincere Churchman might grieve over a son, or nephew, who had lapsed into dissent. Indeed, in the old Squire's eyes radicalism was very little better than Methodism itself, for he was a staunch Churchman.

' I hope not, Jack; but you know there are some matters on which we do not see things alike.' He knew quite well what his uncle meant. 'I don't mean to say that you have not to have your own opinions. God forbid. But you see in poor Earnshaw's case what the Chartist movement really means. "It is a child that is stained with the blood of its mother." I forget who said that; but it is true! The Whigs advanced to violence to get reform; and the Chartists are treading in the same steps. The demand for reform has one leg planted on violence, and the other on agitation. The agitation covers the other.'

'But the real serious reformers among the Chartists utterly disapprove of the "physical force" men. Ask old Jim Woodcock what he has to say about it!'

'Old Jim Woodcock is a Chartist; and Dan Appleyard is a Chartist; and more lawless fellows than Dan are Chartists. For that matter the offscourings of the country everywhere are Chartists. And mob law will carry the day. Indeed if there be any law left at all; mob or other.'

'That the Chartist movement is clogged by the riotous element joining it, is a fact; and a very unfortunate fact. Further, however reasonable the real reformers may be, they are overwhelmed in the towns by the excitable young fellows whose minds run on physical force and pikes. There is no place where that is better seen than in Sheffield. More's the pity.'

'It is rumoured that it was probably some Sheffield ruffian that murdered Tom Earnshaw in that dastardly way. I told Jim Woodcock that assassination was not the way to reform. I gave him a bit of my mind.'

'And how did Jim take it?'

'He turned on me firmly and respectfully till I was obliged to apologize to the old man.'

'That was like you, uncle. Ever the same. But you see, Jim, as one Chartist, could not hinder another man who happens to have joined the Chartist movement, from murdering Earnshaw as a matter of private revenge.'

'May be. But if this kind of violence has to be tolerated by the better men for the sake of "the cause;" I think the cause had better be abandoned altogether.'

'I don't quite see that, uncle. I do not see why men like Jim Woodcock, who would vote as conscientiously as you or myself, should be deprived of their right to a voice in the councils of the nation, because a lawless set of fellows will break the law.'

'But if you enfranchise one you must give a vote to the other. If the one will make a good use of it, it is quite as certain the other will make a bad use of it. There is a positive objection to the scheme in that. The fellow that murdered Earnshaw would have as much voice in the election of a member as I have myself. I don't think that agreeable, or, for that matter, desirable.'

John Wharton felt that his uncle had an argument there which could not well be got over. But as the essence of the Charter was the recognition of the equal rights of man, its advocates were bound to be logical : though the clearer-sighted of them had no affection for their ruffian coadjutors.

'The older reformers recognized that factor, and provided against it by not asking the franchise for those "incapacitated by nature for want of reason, or by law from the commission of crime." The real reformers do not wish to be loaded with a dead-weight of ruffianism, that will always try to drag them down; and certainly always hamper them.'

'Then why don't they shake themselves loose from these political associates ? If they dislike them so much !'

'Because they cannot very well do so, it seems.'

'Well, it would speak well for them if they tried. But the whole thing is nothing more than a cloak for lawlessness. Under the cover of agitation, revolution is brooding.'

' I cannot think so. Agitation is the very thing to prevent revolution. Let the people agitate their grievances, and then there will be no July barricades, and revolution such as sent Charles X. out of France in 1830. "The Charter and Liberty" was the cry before the revolution culminated. If we had had George IV. on the throne much longer, the spirit of incense against the Government would have been driven in the direction of revolution in England.'

' That would never have happened. The Duke would have taken care of that. The army would have seen to that.'

' And England been ruled by a military despotism ; and King George have sat on a throne of bayonets.'

This was a decidedly exasperating remark ; and one John Wharton would not have uttered had he had time to think over the matter.

' I never expected to hear a Wharton speak

of his king and crown like that. But now
when there is only a young girl on the
throne sedition is fairly safe.' The ring
of scorn was very distinct in the tones in
which this taunt was uttered.

'Reform is not sedition, uncle. The
people have a right to discuss their rights;
no matter whether a girl or a grown man
sits on the throne of England;' was the
answer very slowly enunciated, telling of
inward anger. It was clear both speakers
were beginning to throw feeling into their
speech. They presented the spectacle of two
perfectly honest persons hopelessly opposed
to each other in thought and feeling.

'We are not to call things by their right
names because they sound unpleasant! Then
we may as well give up the argument at
once. If we have to pick nice words only,
it would be like fighting a battle with
muskets loaded with scented paper instead
of bullets. That is not my style of warfare.
But I am old-fashioned.'

This was said in a less offensive tone, and

John Wharton perceived that his uncle was determined not to yield a point, and yet the contention was clearly distasteful to him. He felt that in their respective positions it was obviously his duty to change the topic, since compromise was evidently out of question. Yet he did not think it well to go too far afield for the new topic.

'" *Tempora mutantur nos et mutamur in illos.*" But what do you say to the new movement which has sprung up in antagonism to the Charter ? '

' What is that ? '

' Have you not seen in the papers an account of a meeting of Free-traders at Manchester, at a dinner given to Dr. Bowring, to agitate against the Corn Laws ? '

' No I haven't; and I am not delighted to hear of it now. Some other scheme on the part of the manufacturers, I'll be bound. They want cheap bread, to lower wages. It is nothing else but selfishness. Another form of opposition to the Government ; an attack on the landed interest.'

' It is a purely Anti-Corn Law Association. It is to have nothing to do with any political matters but its own. It will have nothing to do with the Charter.'

'There is some sense in that, anyhow. They can see the Charter will come to no good. But the movement is hostile to the landowners, and you will be one some day; why, are to some extent now. I hope you will keep clear of that movement, Jack. Your Chartist views are against you, you know, with the Lord-Lieutenant. If it had not been for them you would have been a magistrate before now. It is a great pity you are not on the bench; we want some younger men, like Oldfield.'

' But I cannot allow my personal interests to lead me away from my duty as a man. All laws are made for the benefit of the people; and the more people are benefited by them the better the laws, I take it.'

' And therefore you think the multitude are to be preferred to the aristocracy. The few have led the many in the past; and look

what England has become!   What has done
so well in the past has a claim to our consideration.   It is a good thing to let well alone.'

'But the Corn Laws are of recent origin.
It does not seem to me fair to tax the
people in so terrible a manner in order to
protect the land.'

'But the land bears the burdens.   It
always has done.   Rent took the place of
military service in the old days.   And in
the long war with Napoleon, the land had
to find the soldiers, and the money for them
too.   The Corn Laws protect the land, and
so the farmers can pay their rent.'

'But it is very hard for a poor man to
see his children crying with hunger when
his wages will not allow him to buy the
taxed bread.'

'What is the tax on corn at present?'

'It is only a trifle.   Corn is so dear.'

'Very well, it is not the tax that makes
bread dear.   What is a duty of one shilling
a quarter on corn?   How much dearer does
that make a quartern loaf?'

'It does not make one loaf appreciably dearer. But it is reducing the country to starvation all the same.'

'How do you make that out?'

'Because the corn-duty deters the foreign wheat-growers from growing wheat for the English market. They never know what the demand may be; nor what the duty will be.'

'And we are to benefit the foreign growers at the expense of the English farmers? Is that your argument?'

'That is not so much the question, uncle, as how our suffering poor are to be fed. When wages were good, and harvests were good, there was no pinch in spite of the speculations of the corn-merchants. But want is at the bottom of the disquiet around us.'

'Want has been felt before. It is the seditious crew of agitators who fan the passions of the people; till they feel their hunger all the keener. You can't agitate to regulate the weather. Bad harvests depend upon bad seasons. The farmers and the landowners can't help that.   Can they?'

'Certainly not.'

'But the manufacturers can help the bad wages.   They have overstocked the markets ; they have taken advantage of machinery, and overdone the markets. That is their fault.   You cannot deny that!'

'But no one proposes to tax inventions in order to protect the hand workers.'

'No ; the manufacturer knows his own interest too well for that. He does not want to check the inventors of labour-saving machines. Not he. That is not his game. He wants to lower the price of food, so that the labourer's wages may go so much further. He knows which side his bread is buttered on. He tells us free-trade would open foreign markets to his goods. That is what he wants with the removal of the corn-tax.'

'He certainly does not affect not to have a personal interest in the doing away of the corn-laws. He says free-trade would help him in these days of slack trade. If the

United States could exchange their corn, on fair terms, for English manufactures, then corn would come in freely, and the workman have a cheap loaf; while the manufacturer would do more trade and could pay more in wages.'

'Ay, that is his specious way of putting it. But don't you see the land would suffer all the same; the land would be worth so much less.'

'Then let the land grow something else than corn.'

'That is all very well for you who grow no corn. Your land is suited for grazing; and Ellwood is a capital judge of lean stock. He knows what will fatten readily, and so pay you. It's Ellwood's judgment that makes the Grange Farm pay. That's what it is.'

'I do not deny that without judgment in the purchase of stock no grazing farm could pay. But that does not imply that the English farmer should go on ploughing his land, because he does not know what else to do with it.'

'But his lease binds him down to a certain plan of culture; tells him what to do. He has his land on these terms.'

' Then alter the leases and let him do as he likes with the land; provided he pays his rent, and keeps his land in good condition.'

This was a terribly destructive doctrine. The landowners had found it desirable to lay down certain courses of crops in their leases for the guidance of tenants; and perhaps when the landlord's agent was far ahead of the agriculturist in knowledge, it was a good plan for all; but it is clear that a rigid course of crops irrespective of seasons and weather must entail a certain element of unfitness in some seasons. The existence of the corn-laws encouraged such paternal guidance, which smacked of feudal times. The whole scheme of legislation was to protect the land; both those who owned it, and those who tilled it.

'Do away with the terms of leases? Is that the next move in contemplation? I think we are coming to a pretty pass. To do away with the corn-laws! to help the foreign grower! A cheap loaf to eke out bad wages; and the abolition of courses in leases to follow; and, to crown all, mob-law! 'Pon my word, Jack, this is queer talk in Gaythorne Hall; such talk as I never expected to hear. And what do you think has to come of us all if these views are taking hold of the country?' The Squire recoiled at the prospect, which certainly had no charms for him. 'And then the railways coming; horse-breeding will be knocked on the head. A farmer had a brood mare or two, and a good coach-horse at five years old was worth thirty pounds: it left him a fair profit. Now soon there will be neither coach-horse nor stage-waggon-horses wanted; only hunters. The ordinary farmer will never breed hunters to a profit. They cannot all turn graziers as you are, even if they could judge stock. I don't see what is to become of the land; that I don't.'

The Squire was growing angry again.

'It is just the old story over again; that balancing of the interests of class against class, that has been the bane of the land. The wiseacres of the fifteenth century put a tax on foreign corn to encourage corn-growing, and help the agricultural labourer against the wool-grower; who employed comparatively few field-hands. Then they taxed wool for exportation, to encourage the clothmaker. Then wool accumulated, and there was bad trade. The wool-grower could not pay his rent; and landlords being legislators they tinkered at the laws again. This mending and tinkering never succeeded; the land has never prospered when swaddled in this way. Propped up and bolstered by time-serving legislation, the land was badly cultivated. If it was left to itself, it would flourish far better.'

This severe and, to the Squire, hostile criticism of the wisdom of his ancestors, directly impugned the whole of paternal legislation, and of the capacity of the few to legislate for the many. It smelled of the

Charter and universal suffrage; and the smell was most offensive in the nostrils of a Tory squire. He could say little: but perhaps on that very account he felt the more.

'To think it should come to this! Oh, Jack, are these the views of the next Squire of Gaythorne Hall?'

The tones were those of sorrow rather than anger. The Squire's benign features had lost their kindly look, and taken on an aspect of sternness. A species of horror had seized upon him.

His nephew had said what he felt, and he could not retreat from what he had said. He had spoken his mind; he could not withdraw a word that he had said. Great as was his love for his uncle; his respect for him; unwilling as he was to give him pain; he could not unsay what he had said.

'I am sorry to grieve you, uncle; but a man has his convictions.'

'Yes, Jack; and your convictions are not mine. I cannot think what the country will come to if the next generation of country squires take to thinking as you do; the country will go to wreck and ruin.'

'I sincerely trust not, uncle. I am not so afraid of the consequences of public reform.'

'Well, I am afraid of them. I said before, a Wharton should never be afraid of anything but not doing his duty. But I have grave fears as to the consequences of this agitation. We shall see some dreadful catastrophe happen, I fear. If there is another bad harvest next year there is no saying what may happen.'

His nephew felt a strong inclination to answer that the best thing to be done was to abolish the corn-laws; so that if a short harvest did come, then there would not be famine. But he saw his uncle was hurt; and so, by a strong exercise of will, he refrained from saying what he felt sorely tempted to say.

'For the sake of the country at large, I sincerely trust we will not have a bad harvest again soon. There will be terrible misery; and, what is more, what misery leads to,—if our next harvest is no better than the last.'

' We are in agreement there, Jack,' said the Squire, in tones telling of his recovery of his temper; which he had been very near losing.

'What do you think Edie will do about Oldfield, Jack, if he was to ask her again ? I hope her answer is not final ?'

' I am sure I cannot say, uncle. I don't think she has any strong feeling about him. She seems friendly enough. But, you know, she is not the girl to marry on a mere feeling of friendliness. She is in no haste to be married, I fancy.'

' I wish it were settled, Jack. If she was married to a safe, steady-going fellow like Oldfield, I should feel easy about her future.'

' What do you mean, uncle ?'

' Why, I mean this : Oldfield is a man we know; a man in a good position ; a steady, trustworthy fellow, who would take care of her. There is a sense of fitness in the match.'

'I do not feel such confidence in Oldfield myself. He is very sagacious about criticizing other people, and showing how they made their mistakes; but he may make a mistake himself some day. He has put his foot deep into that Wybrow Bank business. If bad harvests come he may find his foot further in than is pleasant.'

'I think he is all right. The Bank pays well, he tells me.'

'But you would have nothing to do with it yourself, when it was started.'

'Ah, that was quite a personal matter; I could not stand Waddington. A Wharton is apt to be touchy; and when we met he carried things with such a high hand, that I could have nothing to do with him. My touchiness has kept a lot of money out of my pocket. I know that.'

'If anything went wrong with Waddington, or Mortlake, the two largest shareholders, Oldfield might find himself in an awkward fix. He and the others might find themselves with their fingers badly burned.'

'I don't think there is much likelihood of that happening. There is a risk, no doubt, but not a valid one, of things going wrong. But Oldfield is a man of stability in every way. You see, Edie is a bit like yourself, Jack. She does not hold on to the safe lines of the past. She will act for herself. We have seen that in the district visiting. Now, if she was married to Oldfield she would be safe. He would see she followed the regular rules of other women.'

'Perhaps Edie is not so anxious to be reined in, uncle.'

'Possibly not ; but it would be a comfort to me to know she was settled. You see your tastes and ways run off from what has been the rule with the Whartons. You make new friends, and Edie is only young. If she was to take a fancy to one of your Radical friends, she might be headstrong, and marry him. And this might not be a good connection for the family. If she was married to Oldfield such a thing would be out of the question.'

Jack felt all that was implied in this speech: all the distrust of his views in this danger of his sister marrying some one of like views. It involved, too, the suggestion that Edith might forget what was due to the Wharton family. He was angered at his uncle; and yet he felt the view was the only one the old Squire could be expected to hold. He could see that clearly enough.

'I can see what you mean, uncle,' he answered. 'But I think we can trust Edie. We have unfortunately not been able to see many things in the same light this morning, uncle; we are not usually so unfortunate. I hope next time our talk will be more harmonious. Good morning, uncle; I hope the gout will be better soon.'

With this John Wharton took his departure, saying, 'Gout makes him crusty!' The old Squire moved his gouty foot about uneasily, and looked steadily into the fire.

'Harmony indeed! It seems to me we get further away from it all along the line; and not nearer. Jack evidently does not care about Oldfield for a brother-in-law. Edie will be taking a fancy to some of those Radical friends of Jack's before long, or I am mistaken. It will be a deuced pity if she does. I wish she was Mrs. Oldfield, and an end made of it.'

CHAPTER III.

THE RESULTS OF FROST.

EARLY in January, 1839, a great hurricane occurred in which some of the new steam-packets beginning to run across the Atlantic from the Mersey, were wrecked ; and much damage was done on land. Shortly after that frost came, and held his ground till all around Brigstone was ice-bound.

There is something wonderfully exhilarating about a continued frost, especially if it be accompanied by bright weather. Whether it is that some deep-buried feelings handed down from our old Norse ancestors come to the surface then ; some old-world sympathy with its surroundings getting uppermost ; or a suspension of ordinary occupations leads to the adoption of some substitute with the

high animal spirits engendered by bright
cold, or what; certain it is that a spell of
frost seems to start a new life all its own.
Comforters, mittens, muffatees, straw bands
round the legs, winter apparel belonging to
all classes, according to their means and
condition, appear with a profusion which
strikes one forcibly. The urchins turn out
in force, the iron rims of the wooden-soled
clogs enabling them to slide upon the ice
with the greatest facility. How carefully
does each little fellow nurse his ' calkers,' as
these iron rims are locally designated, when
the time of frost comes near; so as to have
a fine smooth surface, free from any projecting nail-heads, with which to glide easily
over the glassy surface of the frozen water;
and how great is his chagrin if by any
accident the iron rim becomes injured so as
to need repair, with its resultant rough
surface! New clogs are much prized at any
other time; but are decidedly at a discount
when Jack Frost puts in an appearance.
And at high-lying Brigstone the frost was

apt to take a firm hold, and to continue for some time. Slides were made on which the urchins followed one another with ceaseless activity. Boys rarely act in unison, or in order, without much ado and no little noise; but whether shouting possesses less of its charms when the air is cold, or that inexplicable something born of frost comes into play with them or not, slides seem to possess some wonderful disciplinary power. The little fellows arrange themselves in order with marvellous readiness. A little run to gain the requisite impetus, and away goes the aspirant to sliding-fame, balancing himself cautiously as he glides over the slippery slide. Many an unsuccessful essay ends in a fall, which is rarely severe enough to cause more than a disturbing sense of failure. Hour after hour flies away, and meal-times are cut down to the minimum of time. A few hasty mouthfuls are all that can be taken, in order to lose as little as possible of the precious sliding. As soon as day dawns some of the most adventurous spirits are seen inspecting the condition of the slides with a critical eye. When darkness falls, most unwillingly are the slides abandoned for a warm meal, and then bed: for slides are sleepy things. Good housewives meet the strain upon the meal-hours by lavish quantities of toffy. And what North-country boy was ever happier than when he possessed at once a good long slide and a good store of toffy in his pockets, within easy reach of his mittened fingers? Not even snow, with its rough charm of snowballing, can compare with the slide for its complete captivation of the boyish mind. When there is ice, snow is voted a nuisance; and a snowball just landed in the neck is not refreshing when the glee of sliding is at its height; and a quarrel is felt to be inconvenient and out of place; for ice, somehow, among its other physical effects, seems to lessen the pugnacity of small boys, while snow takes the direction of bloody noses.

The great scene of activity for the junior members of the village community of

Brigstone, at this time, was the long dam above the grist-mill. Here slides were formed on the surface of the dam; while the smallest or more timid children sat or stood on the edges; looking on with a sense of envy at the prowess or the courage of those who slided along with balanced bodies and up-held hands. Girls do not show to advantage upon the ice; and in this, their unfitness for boyish sports is once more manifested. Whether from timidity, natural awkwardness, or the effect of ice upon the female mind, girls make a maximum of shouting to a minimum of sliding, constantly falling. Even when two boys take each a hand, and drag her with her iron-shod clogs along the slide, a girl cuts no figure, either imposing or becoming. It is only when skates are reached that the female prowess on ice is shown to advantage.

Clad in furs, their hands buried deep in a warm muff, the gay Viennese girls glide swiftfully and gracefully over the ice; many expert skaters, unrivalled unless it be by the Canadians. The 'inside edge,' the 'outside edge,' 'figure cutting,' all the accomplishments of the adept, are to be seen among the female as well as the male skaters on the *eislanf verein* near the Ring. Wonderful feats of agility are performed by the more famous or ambitious youths; and who can recall his experiences on the ice there without smiling at the remembrance of some youth narrowly escaping a fall, —which might have resulted in breaking his neck,—drawing himself up and looking around for the meed of admiration at his feat? What human figures are more graceful, or what movements so easy, as those of a trio of Viennese girls, hand in hand, gliding swiftly over the rink? Constant long frosts make them experts; as frost makes experts elsewhere.

Skating was not a common accomplishment at Brigstone, and consequently the popular interest of the juveniles centred in slides. For these the long dam of the mill was the scene of their activity and their energies. The large weir above the dam was the attraction rather of the adults. Here the few who possessed the art of skating disported themselves; while the bulk present were mere onlookers.

The weir was a considerable pool, some hundred yards across, and some hundred and fifty from the dam at the bottom to the sedges at the top; the feeding-stream being but a narrow streak. It lay east and west; while its southern shore consisted of a wood chiefly of oak, with a few firs and alders near the edge. The northern shore was fairly clear of trees, except a clump of alders. The southern shore sloped sharply down to the water's-edge; and consequently betwixt the bank and its trees the sun was cut off from the weir, until it had worked round somewhat to the west. Until then the pool was dark and sombre, with scarcely a human being on its surface. But after midday a skater or two appeared as the sun got on the icy surface. Onlookers gathered, creeping down through the wood, lining the rocks on the southern shore near the dam, or clustering on the dam itself. The sluice (or 'shuttle' as it is locally called) was held fast in the grip of Jack Frost; but formed a temptation to many of the men to try their strength, by seeing if they could move it. When the weir was frozen it was an event at Brigstone; certainly a sort of afternoon half-holiday for the men of all conditions. Of course the other sex would be present too; and much genial good-natured laughter told of the enjoyment of the unwonted scene of persons on the weir-pool.

Among those present one afternoon were John Wharton and his sister. The latter was an accomplished skater; and nothing impressed the good folks of Brigstone more with the sense of that lady's superiority to those of her sex around her, than her proficiency on the ice, where all others were so inconspicuous. Mrs. Pryor did not skate; nor as a Rector's wife had she any desire to acquire this particular accomplishment.

One other lady only was there on the pool
who could skate. The attention of the
onlookers was divided between these two
unfamiliar objects, viz., ladies skating.
Their local pride was touched to see that
Miss Wharton was unquestionably the more
proficient skater of the two.

John Wharton skated well too; for he
had skated over most of the Netherlands at
one time or another. He loved to practise
the 'Dutch-roll,' leaving behind him the
calliper-like lines on the ice which reminded
him of the Dutch women skating to market;
contrasting strongly with the divergent
finish of the stroke found in ordinary
skating.

There were several other gentlemen on
skates, and among them George Ashworth,
the surveyor, who used to visit at Fowrass
Grange some time before; when surveying
the projected route of the Manchester and
Sheffield railway. He, too, was an expert
on the ice, and very graceful his tall, lithe
figure looked as he sped along. He had

learned to skate in the Fens, where speed is
the great end aimed at. Men, famous local
skaters, from other parts of England, strive
in vain with the fen-skaters as they fly past
Crowland on the broad surface of the Wel-
land; and soon cease striving, hopeless of
success. His great power and high spirit
were never more conspicuous than upon
the ice, and he could easily distance any
other skater on the weir-pool. He and
John Wharton greeted each other most
cordially when they met again; while Miss
Wharton was as friendly as of yore, her
greeting being quite unembarrassed by any
troublesome remembrance of former days.
It was purely and genuinely friendly. As to
George Ashworth, he thought Miss Wharton
all the handsomer for the lapse of time, in
her completer womanliness. Four years of
earnest life had but developed her loveli-
ness. A tall, graceful, active figure she
looked in her warm dark dress, and her
sealskin hat and muff. The exercise and
the cold had together called up some colour

on her ordinarily pale features. He addressed her as Miss Wharton ; in some doubt, however, as to whether she might not have changed her name. It was scarcely likely that she had become Mrs. Oldfield, without his being aware of it ; but he had been away surveying for a time in the West of England, and this might have occurred in his absence. 'You are a competent skater, I observe,' he said in complimentary tones. ' A rather rare female accomplishment up here, I should think.'

' To judge from those present you are quite right. The other lady is evidently a beginner. But she promises well.'

' Yours is no recent acquisition then ? '

' Oh no. I used to skate when a little girl.'

' Do you get much practice up here ? '

' Not much. One just gets to feel at home on the ice when it is gone. And a second frost sufficient for skating rarely comes ; and when it does, it is gone directly. It is rather chilly standing ; I will take another turn.' And so Miss Wharton left the group, and went scudding away at great speed. George Ashworth looked after her with a long steady look. His dark eye dilated as he watched the graceful figure. What he may have thought it is impossible to say ; but his remark, 'I beg your pardon,' to an observation from John Wharton, told that his ear had not caught the words.

'I asked if you remembered our old evening chats at Fowrass Grange ?' repeated John Wharton.

'I should think I do. What enjoyable evenings they were, to be sure. How I used to think over them when alone in the West, surveying for a line to Gloucester.'

'That is how you have been engaged since we lost sight of you ? My sister from time to time used to ask me, " Do you ever hear anything of Mr. Ashworth now ? " But I was never able to give her an affirmative answer.'

George Ashworth felt a sudden thump, not very violent, but unmistakable, over that area where most men wear their watches. Why did Miss Wharton ask after him? Did she too look back upon those evenings? if so, with what feelings? He would have liked to have asked if Miss Wharton was engaged to Mr. Oldfield; but felt he could not ask her brother. Their position would not warrant that. Such an inquiry would have been highly improper. Still he did wonder.

'Shall we take a turn round the weir?' asked John Wharton, 'for the wind is keen.'

'By all means.' They set off, and skated easily over the pond, round and round, chatting freely.

'This is better than standing still. I wonder how the crowd keep warm?'

'Don't you see? they keep together. A crowd can keep itself warm. Are you interested in the Anti-Corn Law movement at all? Do you think of attending the meeting at Sheffield on the 28th, in answer to the Manchester meeting?' asked Ashworth, rather eagerly.

' Then you have not lost any of your old political fervour. Have you taken any side with the Chartists ? '

' I have had something else to do. Of course my sympathies are with them. But the scheme is too visionary for my matter-of-fact mind. I like this agitation about the Corn Laws : they are an unmitigated evil. I think the move of Bowring and Cobden a most practical one. They restrict their programme to the repeal of these laws, and will have nothing to do with the Charter. These hard times are in their favour too.'

They were circling round, talking eagerly, and interchanging views ; but George Ashworth's eyes were never far away from the graceful dark figure of Miss Wharton, as she too pursued her own way on the ice. She amused herself by some special performances, after which she struck off in a round of the weir. At the eastern end, where the feeder came in the pool, it was fringed with sedges ; and here was a spring, so that the ice was thin. But the fact was barely known, and Miss Wharton was in ignorance of it. A light youth had skated much nearer the line of sedges than John Wharton and his friend had gone. Ashworth noticed that the ice looked thin, but paid no special attention to the fact. Miss Wharton followed the marks of this skater, and when nearing the sedges she turned to keep clear of them. Unluckily a twig had become embedded in the ice, and her skate cutting into it, she was tripped, and staggered forward to recover herself; the ice gave way, and she disappeared. A cry arose from the crowd.

' Miss Wharton's i' th' watter. T' ice hes broke.'

Ashworth had been following the girl's movements with a persistency only broken by a remark made just then by her brother, which took off his attention. The cry struck his ear; looking up, he saw she had disappeared, and there was a hole in the ice. The situation flashed itself upon him—rather than was the subject of conscious thought.

He struck off without any attempt at explanation, and shot for the broken place. When John Wharton looked up to see why his companion had so abruptly left him, he saw him with his long fen-stroke making for the sedges. At the same moment he realized the meaning of the cry, and saw what had happened. He struck out too; but had not gone far when he saw Ashworth putting down the heels of his skates partly to arrest his speed, partly to break the ice, and, an instant after, go in through it. It was clear he was trying to save the girl. For a moment Wharton's intellect seemed paralyzed by his horror at the danger which his sister was in; but it regained its sway as he saw Ashworth's head rise above the water: it was not so deep as to take Ashworth in over his head. Then the head went down a little, and as he got near he saw Ashworth groping about, and then his sister's head appear. He turned as he neared the spot so as not to break more ice; and his own plunging in was unnecessary, for Ashworth was the taller of the two, despite John Wharton's stature.

'You've got her safe, Ashworth?' he asked.

'Yes, I have her safe. Get a ladder, or something to put across the hole.'

Ashworth's experience in the fens told him what to do in a case of this kind.

'Get a ladder!' Wharton shouted to the crowd on the dam, and away broke several of the men.

'To Joe Hague's for a stee' (north country for a ladder) was the cry taken up.

'Or a plank,' shouted another.

Away they went with willing Yorkshire hearts and sturdy Yorkshire legs.

Joe Hague, the carpenter, was working away steadily in his shop to make up for his son's being at the weir to see the skating. He was surprised by the in-rush of several men panting for breath, two seizing a ladder, while the other two got a plank off the rack, without attempting to ask leave. Among the rest was his own son Tom, who, familiar with all the details of the place, made for a pole sawn up to form the two sides of a ladder. He seized one half, and on his father's shouting,

'What's ta goan to do wi' th' pole, Tom?'

'Miss Wharton's i' th' watter,' was all the reply vouchsafed. 'Tek' houd o' t'uther end,' he said to a companion, and away they went.

Old Joe went to help the others to get a ladder.

'It'll be handier nur a plank. Tom 'll git th' pole across th' hoile, an' then yo' can git th' ladder across. Away wi' yo. Loise no toime, for goodness' seake.'

They lost no time in hurrying off with the ladder; but Tom and his co-worker were half-way back with the half-pole before they could get out of the yard with the ladder. As they were hurrying out they saw Mr. and Mrs. Pryor driving towards them.

' What is the matter ?' asked the Rector.

' Miss Wharton's thro' th' ice,' was the curt reply; and they hastened away with the ladder.

' There's been an accident, Agnes. Let us drive on. We may be able to drive her home. Probably there is no conveyance at hand.'

So saying he touched up the pony, and drove away to that point of the road nearest the weir. The highway went around somewhat, but they were soon there.

' Take the reins while I go to the weir,' said the Rector; handing the reins to his wife with an unceremoniousness very unusual with him.

In the mean time the greatest excitement prevailed at the weir. Some, not knowing what to do, had made for the sluice, with the idea of drawing off the water in the weir, and so lowering it. Even if the sluice would have moved under their strenuous efforts, the outflow would have been perfectly inoperative.

'Up wi' th' shuttle,' was one cry : and right willingly they set to work at their useless effort.

John Wharton kept the crowd back, shouting in stentorian tones :

'Keep back. Keep where you are. Don't crowd on the ice; or you may come in, and make bad worse.'

One or two of the better-dressed helped him to keep order. The light-weight whose thoughtless career had led to the disaster kept hovering about.

'Keep up, sir,' he said to Ashworth. 'They are coming with a ladder. They will be here soon,' he cried.

George Ashworth was keeping up courageously, but the cold of the water was chilling him rapidly. He had scarcely time to gather his wits together when he went into the water overhead. As soon as he got his head above water, he dashed off the muddy water from his eyes and looked about him. The two immersions had stirred up the mud, and the water was

thick, and obscured the view. Groping
about he caught hold of Miss Wharton's
dress, and pulling, drew her from under-
neath the ice, her face blanched with fright.
She seemed to have lost consciousness, and
struggled violently. He felt that he stood
on the soft bottom of the pool, and that
the water was up to his neck. He could
hold her above the water, he saw; for
his wits were quick, and he had been
present at an ice-accident before. So when
John Wharton came near him he was holding Miss Wharton with her head above the
water. He was quite self-possessed, and
having answered Wharton's inquiry, turned
his attention to his fair burden; she was
gasping for breath, and deliriously struggling, for she had drawn in a quantity of
water while under the ice. He grasped
her firmly to prevent her getting from
him; and, as her clothes were soaking in
the water, she grew heavier and heavier.
His standing ground was uncertain, and
his skates cut into the soft bottom of the

weir. He had to shift his feet frequently to prevent his mouth and nose getting under the black water around him ; but the burden gave him energy. Somehow, he was never clear how, it seemed to him that his feelings towards Miss Wharton were warmer, stronger, more intense than he had ever dreamt of, as he held her from sinking into the dark muddy water. This feeling lent him an accession of energy. Having breathed once or twice freely, her consciousness seemed to be returning.

' Oh, where am I ? ' she gasped.

' You're safe. Keep quiet.'

' Who is it ? Where am I ?' she cried, and commenced struggling again; evidently realizing she was in danger, but without any definite idea of its nature.

She nearly escaped his grasp, and, as it was, drew his face below the water ; but by a strenuous effort he maintained both his grip and his standing-ground.

He was beginning to feel the strain on him when a loud shout coming from the crowd, gave him encouragement to hold on. Then John Wharton and the light-weight skater might have been seen making away from the crowd, and hurrying over the weir to the scene of the accident. Approaching, John Wharton cried :

'Do you see the pole, Ashworth ?'

'Yes,' was the reply.

'Then we will push it towards you. Lift the end so as to get it over the ice on the other side.'

The pole was pushed towards him, and he gave the end the desired lift, while Wharton and his helper pushed it well over the broken edges of the ice.

'Hurra !' shouted Wharton. 'Now you can rest on the pole.'

And Ashworth got one arm over the pole, and supported himself and his burden.

'The ladder is coming directly. Can you hold on now ?'

'Famously !'

'Then hold on a bit longer ;' and so

saying, John Wharton went back to the lower end of the weir.

Ashworth now had time to pay more attention to his helpless burden. He was no longer afraid of her struggles forcing both under water; so he tried to recall her consciousness.

'Miss Wharton!' he said, in deep tones.

'What?' cried the girl wildly.

'Don't you know me?'

'No. Who are you? What are you doing?'

It might not have been very easy for her to have recognized George Ashworth just then, even if she had been in full possession of her faculties. The black muddy water rendered him unrecognizable; especially to her disordered mind, still palsied by the shock.

'I am George Ashworth. I am holding you up from drowning.'

'From drowning? I am in the water? And she stared with wide-open eyes at him, her blanched face discoloured by the dirty water.

'You are safe now.'

'Am I? But oh, it is so cold!' she said slowly and with difficulty. 'Are you not cold?' she asked wearily.

'Rather. But help is at hand. Here is your brother coming with a ladder.'

She turned in the direction indicated, and then, her eyes closing, her head dropped upon his shoulder.

The situation was most uncomfortable in every way: how was it then that George Ashworth felt as if he would not exchange his position for any other upon earth?

CHAPTER IV.

THE RESCUE.

HE was soon, however, again to use his utmost energies; the ladder was brought along the ice by two men who relieved the others who brought it, for they were out of breath with their exertions. Under John Wharton's directions they got it near the broken place, when he said:

'Now, put it down, and both of you push it endwise across the hole. Keep it on the other side of them, away from the pole.'

They did so: and George Ashworth found that he could rest on the ladder on one side, and upon the pole on the other.

'Can you hold on any longer?' asked John Wharton.

'I think so; but I am getting chilled.'

Though they had thus got a ladder across on one side, and the pole on the other, there remained the difficulty of getting at them immersed in the water. John Wharton had his skates on, he therefore could not stand upon the ladder. Ashworth saw the difficulty, and cried :

'Let one of the men creep along the ladder.'

One of the men then crept along the ladder, until he reached Mr. Ashworth.

'Take hold,' the latter said. 'Take firm hold, now;' as he raised the unconscious form until the man had caught the upper portion of her jacket.

'Now pull;' and as the man did so, Ashworth made an immense effort to lift her, and she was got out upon the ice.

'Now then, draw her along a yard or two.'

The man did as he was bid; and soon Miss Wharton, wet, bedraggled, unconscious, but safe, was once more on strong ice.

Her brother felt a huge spasm of satisfaction on being able to look upon her again ; but now came the turn of her preserver.

The man again crept out along the ladder until he could catch hold of George Ashworth's hand.

'Giv' me yer hand,' he said.

But George Ashworth found this by no means so easy to do. He was supporting himself by an arm each over the ladder and the pole. He tried to reach out a hand ; but he could scarcely move.

"Yo're numbed wi' th' cauld, I reckon,' said the man. 'I'll get houd of yor coit-collar.'

So saying, he stretched himself out along the ladder, and catching firm hold of the coat-collar, he pulled with all his might. Ashworth's clothes were soaked with water, which made him heavy even in the water. When the attempt was made to raise him out of it, the weight told. The effort failed.

'Can't yo mek' an effort?' asked the man.

'I'm afraid I can't,' was the reply. 'I'm stiff with cold.'

'So yo er' loike: but wait. I'll tek' anuther grip.'

So setting himself firmly on the ladder, he shouted to his companion:

'Houd th' stee stiddy, Tim; else I can't houd my grip.'

His mate caught good hold of the ladder.

'Noo then, sir. Come along,' he said to Ashworth, who did what he could to help. After a strenuous effort the man drew him forward on to the ladder. He saw, however, that he was too benumbed to make any further effort, and stopped.

'Get me on the ladder, and then pull it away,' he got out feebly.

The man got him on the ladder, and said:

'Yo're out o' th' hoile now. Can yo stop thear, sir, if I loive ye to yersen?'

'Yes; pull away.'

The man crept back to the sound ice, and, joining his mate, the two pulled hard on the ladder, and drew it and Ashworth away from the broken ice.

In the mean time the Rector had had Miss Wharton taken away to the pony-carriage, and driven off to Fowrass Grange by Mrs. Pryor. He himself went again to the weir, and found Mr. Ashworth the object of the most solicitous care. He was cold and almost speechless, and grew colder each moment.

'Has any one anything warm?' asked the Rector. A well-dressed man offered his flask of brandy. The Rector took the flask, and poured some of the fluid betwixt the chattering teeth. The strong man whose courage and energy had so recently been the admiration of all, was now helpless enough himself.

'Take him up to the Rectory, and put him to bed,' was the next idea of the Rector. 'He will soonest come round in a warm bed. Just fasten him to the ladder, and then four of you can bear him along.' Four willing bearers were readily found, and soon the exhausted man was borne away.

The Rector then turned to John Wharton, who was getting off his skates as rapidly as possible.

'Mrs. Pryor is driving your sister home ; I think she is all right, except the ducking. Ashworth is being taken to my house to be put to bed.   It has been a narrow affair.'

'If Ashworth had not plunged in after her she must have been drowned.   The water was up to his chin, and she must have gone down over-head.   Even I could not have saved her.'

'It was a most providential thing there was so tall a man at hand.   Stature is a blessing at times ;' said the Rector, in tones as if thinking aloud.   'You will at once go after your sister, and I will look after Mr. Ashworth.'

'But that looks so selfish after his courageous act.   It will look as if I did not properly estimate the value of his services ; and the risk he ran.   If the water had been a little deeper, both must have perished.'

'I fear so. We have much to be thankful for in the result. I will explain to him.' So the Rector left John Wharton, and turned to the ladder and its burden. The water dripped from the prostrate form, as the men hurried along with their awkward burden. The Rector overtook them, and asked.

'Are you very cold, Mr. Ashworth?'

'Rather,' was the reply through the chattering teeth. The Rector took off his overcoat, and threw it over him. Then encouraging the bearers to further efforts, he said :

'You will soon be in a warm bed. I will hasten on and tell them to get it ready.' So he set off at a brisk pace. By this time Brigstone was alive like a swarm of bees, with the news that Miss Wharton had gone through the ice. Children had carried the news home, and it had spread from house to house. Several women had rushed to Joe Hagues, to learn if Joe could tell them anything.

'Nay, what I knaw naught abaht it. They just coméd for th' stee: an' Tom ran off wi' a powle. That's o' I knaw.' No information could Joe afford. But when they saw the Rector hurrying along, they asked curtly:

'Is Miss Wharton seafe?'

'She is,' was the equally curt reply: the Rector could not stop to explain.

Then they saw the men with the ladder and its burden.

'Wheah is that you've gotten on th' stee?' they asked.

'Mr. Ashworth, wheah seaved her fra' drooning.'

'Bless him! I whope he's na warse,' was the kindly comment. 'The bonniest lass far an' wide.' The bearers went on without delay, and soon got to the Rectory. Here the nearly frozen man was quickly put to bed, with a warm bottle to his feet, and considerable hot fluid internally.

The crowd at the weir were all excitement; and one man saw his way to a guerdon by carrying the news of the accident and the rescue to Gaythorne Hall. Squire Wharton would be glad to know his niece was safe. The rest were all on the move; some venturing up towards the hole.

'Eh, leuk at th' hoile i' th' ice. An' th' black watter. Eh, but it wor a narrow chance,' was the comment of the visitors to that part of the weir.

'Keep away, else you may break in too,' was the advice of a gentleman in the crowd; advice not very readily taken. Everywhere the talk was of the accident, and the brave rescue; Mr. Ashworth's courage being greatly admired.

'He wor so shairp ovver it too. He nivver waited a minute. It'll not be th' first accident he's bin in, I'se warrant,' said one elderly man. 'It's many a year sin thear's bin an accident i' th' weir. I can just remember ane afoar. Sum childer were drooned.'

'He is a grand tall chap, else he nivver cud hav kep his heed aboon th' watter.'

'It wor a rare coud job, I'll be bun',' said another.

'I wonder what Squire Oldfield 'll say to this job?' asked another of speculative turn.

'Aye, it's a spoke i' his wheel, or I'm mistekken,' was the comment of one vinegar-faced old dame, who had come to see the skating; her curiosity having over-mastered her acquisitiveness, and led her away from her spinning-wheel—and who all the while grudged the time she was wasting.

'He'll be i' noa hurry to ask efter th' gentleman 'at seaved her.'

Such and such like was the conversation which went on till the oncome of darkness drove all home, to talk the subject over more leisurely by a warm fireside.

John Wharton soon got to Fowrass Grange, and ascertained that his sister was warm in bed, and comfortable; though of course still excitable.

'What a noble man Mr. Ashworth is!' she said to her brother. 'If it had not been for him I must have been drowned.'

'I am afraid that would have been the case, Edie. There was not another man in the crowd of his inches. His head was barely above the water.'

'How good of him! I can't get my ideas clear about what happened.'

'Well, don't bother about it now. Keep quiet; that is the best thing, is it not, Mrs. Pryor?'

'Most certainly. What has become of Mr. Ashworth?—was that not the name of the gentleman who saved her?' asked Mrs. Pryor.

'He was carried off on the ladder to the Rectory, under the supervision of your husband.'

'I hope you thanked him for me, John. I quite forgot, they hurried me away. I am ashamed of myself.'

'The Rector said he would see to all that; he sent me here to see after you.'

'But will not that look as if we did not appreciate Mr. Ashworth's services?'

'I represented that, but it was no use. I think now you are all right, I will step over to the Hall, and tell uncle. He will be anxious to know all.'

'Give him my love, Jack! and tell him I feel all right, only a little nervous.'

'I will carry your message safely. Will you sit with her while I am away, Mrs. Pryor?'

'Certainly. I will not leave her till you come back.'

As John Wharton walked over from Fowrass Grange to Gaythorne Hall, the events of the day came up vividly before him. Their anticipation of a pleasant afternoon's skating; their utter freedom from the anticipation of any accident; the sudden emergency, and his sister's providential escape; his accidental *rencontre* with George Ashworth; the resumption of their old acquaintanceship under such startling circumstances: all passed through the brain,—the thoughts following each other like coursers in a race. One thing was very clear : if it had not been for Ashworth's stature and capacity, his sister must have been drowned. If he could not have stood on the bottom of the Weir, no man could have kept himself up; let alone another person, with the water soaking into his clothes, and the cold benumbing him. All this went backwards and forwards in his mind, and then came the thought leaping suddenly into his consciousness :

'Ashworth and Edie always got on well together, and she is not the girl to owe her life to a man, and forget him. I think I can see a new complication springing up that will upset Oldfield's calculations. It is scarcely my business; but I would sooner have a manly fellow like Ashworth for a brother-in-law than a little, proper, formal fellow like Oldfield. But I must neither make nor meddle. Uncle Edward will not look at the matter in my light. I may make myself sure about that.'

When he arrived at the Hall it was clear

that news of the event had got there before
him.

'How is Miss Edith?' asked Bulman,
as he opened the door.

'Then you have heard what has happened?'

'Yes; as soon as Miss Edith was safe, a
man came hot-foot to the Hall to tell your
uncle.'

'How very considerate of him; considerate in every way! How is my uncle?'

'A little excited, sir.'

With that John Wharton was shown into
his uncle's sanctum.

'Well, Jack, this has been an eventful
day. How is Edie?'

'She is comfortable in bed, thank you.
I left her under Mrs. Pryor's safe supervision. She sent her love to you; and told
me to tell you she felt all right, only a
little nervous.'

'She is a brave girl, Edie; but she has
had a narrow escape. Who is the gentleman that saved her? The messenger was

not quite sure. He said he was a stranger to these parts.'

'He is George Ashworth, a surveyor. He was in the neighbourhood a few years ago,—surveying the Manchester and Sheffield line; we saw something of him at that time. He came occasionally to Fowrass Grange in an evening.'

'Humph,' said the Squire. Somehow the information did not seem particularly acceptable to him. 'Then he is not quite a stranger? What sort of a man is he? Can I invite him to dinner?'

'I should think so, uncle. His father is a Lincolnshire clergyman.'

The old Squire seemed greatly puzzled.

'You see, Jack, it is rather a difficult matter to decide upon. One does not want to seem indifferent in a matter of this kind; and yet one does not want to receive the man with open arms, without knowing something about him. The Whartons do not take up with anybody.'

'From what I have seen of Ashworth, I

should think he would look upon an invitation to dine with you as rather a formal
acknowledgment of your recognition of his
services. I don't think he would care for
that.'

'People have not been in the custom of
holding an invitation to Gaythorne Hall
cheap; the Whartons have never been
promiscuous in their guests. I suppose I
can hardly send him a cheque; that would
not do.'

The Squire was evidently a little nettled.

'That most certainly would not do!'

'Then I suppose he must have the cap-
tive of his spear and his bow: that is what
it will end in. Edie is just the sort of
romantic girl to throw herself away upon
the man who has saved her life.'

'I don't know that you could call it
throwing herself away in this case.'

'Then I suppose you would have no
objections to her doing so.' This was said
with a very manifest amount of temper.

'If you haven't, I have. She is too fine

a girl to be allowed to dispose of herself as she likes. Others have a right to be consulted in the matter.'

'But, uncle, I do not think Edie is in such a desperate hurry to get married. Why should we discuss that subject; to-day of all days, when she has been so near another destiny?'

'Right, my boy. But you must have a glass of port; we cannot allow the occasion to pass dry-mouthed. Bulman shall un-cork a bottle of 1820, and you shall help me to drink it. Gout, or no gout.'

'How about the gout?'

'I am ever so much better: but gout or not, I am not going to be scared off a glass of port, when my own brother's daughter,—my only niece, Edie, has had so narrow an escape.'

The modern reader will perhaps be shocked at such a heathen way of setting up an Ebenezer; but then they must remember the sort of man Squire Wharton was, and the times.

' I really do not think, uncle, I could do so with a good conscience. I do not think it would do your gout any good.'

' Never you mind, Jack ; I bear the gout, not you! Only mind this : we've got to finish the bottle. The less you drink, the more I must. You must do your fair share under these circumstances.'

' I wish my share fell to a man who appreciated it more.'

' Well, you're no drinker, Jack. Your worst enemy could not charge you with drinking. But to-day remember the occasion. I have sent up word to the Black Swan and the Stanhope Arms to draw a kilderkin of ale each free. I think it a good old-fashioned plan of letting your poorer neighbours share with you in your rejoicings. They enjoy it the more that they have it among themselves.'

' It was very kind of you to do so. I dare say many of them have tasted little all these hard times. But you see only the men benefit by this.'

'That's true; but their wives will be glad to see them merry.'

The teetotal reader must really forgive the old Squire. It was not thought improper for a man to be a little under the influence of alcohol in his rejoicings, in Anglo-Saxon history, up to a period posterior to the times here described.

'There has not been much merriment about lately, certainly. I hope none will drink too much.'

'That will be as it happens. Those who like ale and do not like paying for it, generally show their hand when there is a free cask running. Some fellows, steady as a rule, yield to the temptation. Here comes Bulman.'

The bottle was left, and the Squire induced his unwilling ally to join him with some difficulty.

'Come, Jack, don't hang back. We must drink Edie's health.'

Such was the scene at Gaythorne Hall in the Squire's sanctum. His generosity to

himself and nephew, and to his poorer
neighbours in Brigstone, was extended to
the servants' hall, where some excellent
home-brewed ale was drank to sundry
healths, and sundry songs, under the supervision of Bulman.

Up in Brigstone the ale flowed freely;
and even old Jim Woodcock felt he "must
drink a mug of ale" to Miss Wharton's
health at her uncle's expense; it would not
be neighbourly to abstain from doing so;
though Jim's rule was to drink at his own
expense,—a matter on which he was very
particular.   Perhaps the female sex were
not so entirely excluded from the festivities
as John Wharton had supposed; a quantity
of ale, hot and spiced, was served out in the
kitchens of the two taverns, and discreetly
and moderately tasted out of tea-cups—to
keep up the proper feminine method of
drinking—by some of the wives and daugh-
ters of those who were sitting birling the
ale-cup in the front parlours.   But all was
propriety; for women are not usually seen

now, and certainly were not seen then, in ale-houses in the country.

How and under what circumstances the news of the accident and the rescue reached Orton Hall, and how it was received by its inmates, is not on record. Next day Stephen and Miss Oldfield drove over to Fowrass Grange, and inquired most solicitously about Miss Wharton's condition. John Wharton received them, and informed them that Miss Wharton was pretty well, but was still in bed ; it being thought best for her to remain there, as she still felt a little excited. Miss Oldfield was very impressive about the desirability of her taking every care for a day or two. John Wharton thought it was not a matter for wonder that Miss Oldfield was in general good repute among her sex for kindliness and thoughtfulness.

At the Rectory they all spent a very pleasant evening, for after an hour or two in bed, George Ashworth thought he would like to come down-stairs for a little ; though his host forbade his thinking of leaving the

house. Later in the evening Mrs. Pryor
brought word that she left Miss Wharton
comfortable in bed, and recovering from the
shock.

What were the thoughts of the two chief
actors in the recent incident ?

It is needless to say their thoughts ran
mainly on the danger they had shared
together : of that close identity of interests
which they had divided between them in
the dark icy water of the weir-pool. Miss
Wharton fully realized that without George
Ashworth's help she would never have
emerged from the water a living being ;
that she would have met a watery grave.
By a fortunate accident, George Ashworth
had escaped sharing her fate. Had the
water been deeper, or his stature less, he
must have perished with her, in the attempt
to save her. He had run a terrible risk,
clearly, in adventuring his own life in the
attempt to save hers ; and had been successful ! She owed her life to him. He was
indeed a gallant gentleman, she felt.

George Ashworth's memory recalled with the utmost fidelity every incident, even the most minute, of that experience in the weir-pool. He thought of Miss Wharton's pale, discoloured features ; of the weight of her unconscious form ; of her delirious struggle, when he was compelled to hold her firmly. He felt he would go through it twenty times over, if he might only so hold her in his arms again. It was a delicious memory. Was it a wild hope that he felt surging up in him, that some day, perhaps, he might be able to hold her in his arms again ? What did she think, he wondered ?

Each of them recognized the impression made by a brief but memorable experience. They had been together only some ten minutes ; but already the event seemed indelibly engraved on the life-history of each. Neither could ever forget that time, no matter how brief, when they had been thrown together, isolated from all human contact ; with an experience they shared between them alone, outside the rest of the

world.   When they looked back it was
there: when they thought of the future it
was there.   The impression could never be
effaced.   Come what might, they felt they
could never forget that momentous time.
All their future would carry this impression
with it.   As the great sage says:

'After the tossing half-forgetfulness of
the first sleep that follows such an event,
it comes upon us afresh, as a surprise, at
waking; in a few moments it is old again
—old as eternity.'

These are the brief, impressive moments
which leave their imprint on lives; there
is no more escape from them than that the
body can desert its shadow.   As the sage
continues, he says:

'Did you ever happen to see that most
soft-spoken and velvet-handed steam-engine
at the Mint?   The smooth piston slides
backwards and forwards as a lady may slip
her delicate finger in and out of a ring.
The engine lays one of *its* fingers calmly,
but firmly, upon a bit of metal; it is a coin

now, and will remember that touch, and tell
a new race about it, when the date upon it
is crusted over with twenty centuries.'

The engine of destiny had left its stamp
upon the life-histories of George Ashworth
and Edith Wharton in that brief experience,
—that ten minutes' immersion in the weir-
pool; while Old Death with his scythe was
hovering over them !

CHAPTER V.

A NEW MOVEMENT.

FOR a day or two Miss Wharton remained slightly nervous after her immersion and her escape from death in the weir, but soon she was riding about again on 'Daisy,' eagerly welcomed by all. North country folks are not given to outward demonstrations of class-respect; but the cap was readily doffed, or the old-fashioned curtsey dropped, on her approach.

'God bless yo, Miss! Glad to see yo well again!' was the greeting which met her on all sides; testifying to her popularity with the people around Fowrass Grange. Of course her first ride was to visit her uncle, who was overjoyed to see her after her narrow escape. But his welcome steered clear of all but the barest reference to her preserver. Edith Wharton, woman as she was, saw what that attitude in her uncle meant; it said plainly enough: 'I do not wish to see any one come betwixt Mr. Oldfield and you;' but whether his attitude served his cause, or not, may be open to question.

As to George Ashworth, he called at Fowrass Grange the day after the accident, and found John Wharton at home. He inquired after Miss Wharton, who was in bed. Her brother went up to her, and came back with this message:

'Tell Mr. Ashworth I am well; and thank him for me for saving my life. Perhaps before long I may have an opportunity of thanking him myself.' It was brief, and to the point. Yet it was deliciously sweet to Ashworth's eager ear, in that it referred to the future—to their meeting again. She evidently hoped they would see each other again. A feather will tell which way the wind blows. This reference to the future, slight as it was, fell on Ashworth's ear like a faint distant sound of music only caught by the most attentive listener.

'I am glad to have had the opportunity of being of service to her,' was his remark. Seemingly to get rid of the subject as quickly as might be, he changed the conversation.

'Are you going to attend the meeting at Sheffield on the 28th, Mr. Wharton?'

'The Anti-Corn Law meeting, you mean?'

'Yes. It is called in response to the meetings at Manchester.'

'I shall certainly be there. Have you any idea of the plan of the new movement? It has no connection with the Charter, has it?'

'None whatever. It will have nothing to do with the Chartist, or any other movement. Its sole object is the repeal of the Corn Laws. And for this end it has its own programme of agitation.'

'Have you any idea what proposals will come before the meeting?'

'I fancy the proposition put will be to agitate the subject by meetings and lectures, expounding the facts of the case, and pointing out the injurious effects of the Corn Laws; to have the subject thoroughly ventilated so that the voice of the people will call for their repeal.'

'It seems a most reasonable line to take. I suppose the Chartists will support the movement?"

'I do not know how that may be. The Chartists may support the Anti-Corn Law League; but the League will have nothing to do with the Charter, that is certain. Villiers and Cobden are too clear-sighted to risk their movement by any compromise with the Chartists.'

'I think it might be well to carry something tangible, as well as to advocate reform. But the landowners will fight desperately.'

'That is anticipated, and the measures to

be taken will be proportioned to the opposition looked for.'

'I am glad there is no mistake about the magnitude of what is to be undertaken. Shall you be there?'

'I hope so. If I can manage it, I will: good-bye.'

George Ashworth left Fowrass Grange with a joyous heart. Miss Wharton had expressed the hope of seeing him again. John Wharton's sympathy with the new movement offered a good prospect of his being able to keep up his connection with Fowrass Grange. He carried himself erect; his head thrown back, his shoulders square, his eye looking forward eagerly, as if peering into the future; and looking down the vista, at the end a tall, lithe, female figure could be faintly discerned; his step was elastic and his demeanour buoyant. Hopefulness was manifested in every line of his figure, in every movement.

When the 28th arrived, John Wharton could be seen to mount his powerful steed, equipped for a cold ride. He wore his cord breeches, and riding-boots of stout leather; and a short riding overcoat of thick navy cloth. He looked a country gentleman every inch of him, as he settled down into the saddle easily, and rode off. There was nothing about him to indicate any sympathy with a movement directed straight at the class to which he clearly belonged. Luke Ellwood gazed after him as he rode away.

'He's off to th' meetin' at Sheffield. When th' manufacturers see he's joined them, they'll begin to think th' landowners are comin' ovver to them. But he'll be th' only one thear. That's my opinion. It's a good thing for all on us that th' Grange is a grazing farm.' Whereupon Luke turned away to mind his own duties.

John Wharton enjoyed his ride. Who is there that has been familiar with the circumstances, who does not look back with pleasure to a ride in the morning before the frost has well got off the roads, even where exposed to the sun ?—the bracing air ; the ring of his horse's shoes on the hard, ice-bound road ; the firm feeling of his horse under him, the animal apparently enjoying all as much as his rider. A snort or two testified to the horse's opinion. His rider was too familiar with the scene to be especially impressed. He merely looked round, and remarked to himself that it was a fine winter day, and it was very unlikely the meeting would be interfered with by the elements.

'Come, Hawk,' he said to his horse after awhile, 'you must step out directly. We must be in Sheffield before the hour is over.' Hawk apparently comprehended what was said—as horses often do—and by another snort testified his willingness to increase his pace. As the tall powerful horse with its equally well-built rider rode into the town of Sheffield, their appearance attracted the attention of the gathering crowds.

'He'll be wun o' th' country magistrates comin' to tek' a noat ov' th' meeting, I guess,' was the remark of one of the beholders.

'It's nut th' first day he an' th' herse hav' been out togither, I'se warrant, by th' luik o' them,' said another.

As indifferent to these remarks and the attention he attracted, as complete unconsciousness of both could make him, John Wharton rode to his hostelry; his attention being taken up with the character of the people he saw gathering together for the occasion. They consisted of well-to-do looking men, probably mill-owners and manufacturers, with a large admixture of mill-hands, grinders, operatives, and artisans of the better class. The rough element of the Chartist movement was conspicuous by its absence. He noted this fact, and thought it of good omen.

Soon he reappeared, the traces of travelling having been carefully removed from his boots and outer garments, presenting all the appearance of a gentleman, clad as became his position, and the season. His tall figure could easily be followed amongst the shorter crowd around him.   He had not gone far before he encountered a gentleman whom he knew.

'Why, Wharton, you here?' his acquaintance asked.

'Certainly.   Why not?'

'Why not? Why you are a landowner, and a farmer; the heir to considerable estates; and here at an Anti-Corn Law meeting!'   Turning to a fine grey-haired gentleman with whom he was conversing, he said :

'May I have the pleasure of introducing Mr. John Wharton to you, Mr. Carlyon?'

'Glad to make your acquaintance, Mr. Wharton; from what our common friend here says you could scarcely be expected to come here,—unless it is to take a note of what goes on.'

'I am not only proposing to take a note of the proceedings, but I am decidedly inclined to take a part.'

'Not against us, I hope,' said Mr. Carlyon, rather eagerly.

'No; with you, to be sure! Class interests are strong; and so are individual interests; but national interests are stronger still. I shall need no conversion on the matter of the injurious effects of these Corn Laws; "the bread-tax" they call it in Sheffield.'

'I am delighted to hear you say so. I hope we will have a good meeting. Will you walk on with us?' They turned; the common friend feeling that he had served the part of an intermediary, and was of no farther use. He was not a man given to take offence; and having introduced two men to each other who seemed likely to get on well, he had a pleasant feeling of having done a good turn; and was not inclined to force himself upon their notice. He was gratified to see how genially they took to each other.

Before long they neared the Town Hall, to find that as the day was fine without

any threatening of rain or snow, and the
gathering large, it had been proposed and
carried to hold the meeting in Paradise
Square. So all made for the Square, where
it was understood Colonel Peronet Thompson
was already in his place. The Square was
thronged, and John Wharton's speculations
as to the whereabouts of the Chartists,
moral and physical force both, were solved
by seeing a Chartist banner, or two, surrounded by a dense band of these reformers
in one corner of the Square.

'There are the Chartists, Mr. Carlyon.'

'Ah! so I see. This looks as if they
were going to take some line of their own.'

'The Corn Law agitators are going to
keep clear of the Chartists, I hear?'

'They must, you see. It would be utter
ruin to their cause to be mixed up with
men who have been riotous here and there;
and who, whether they like it or not, have
drawn into their ranks all the seditious
elements over the country, here and elsewhere. They cannot be successful except

by holding aloof completely from any questionable agitation. Villiers and Cobden mean to stick to their last. Corn Law Repeal, pure and simple, is their programme. You will soon hear it expounded.'

It was not long before a clear, powerful, and withal pleasant voice was heard ringing over the large assemblage. This was the gist of what was said :

' It is not necessary to formally introduce the subject of the injurious effects of the Corn Laws to the people of Sheffield. Under your illustrious townsman, Mr. Ebenezer Elliott, an " Anti - Bread Tax Society " has long existed in this town. The agitation for the Reform Bill overwhelmed it, and drew it from its special object. It got caught in the current of the stream of the Reform Agitation ; and it is a lesson to us to avoid the same fate. Another " Anti-Corn Law Association " has been in existence some time in London, of which your townsman, Mr. Roebuck, is a member, as well as other illustrious persons.

They have tried to induce the Government
to promise they will attend to the Corn
Laws ; and the answer has been made them,
that before the Government will do anything they must be convinced that the
voice of the people is in favour of the
repeal of these laws. What does this mean ?
It means that the Government knows that
the House of Commons consists largely of
landowners ; and that, by the property
qualification, every member must have an
interest in the land : while the House of
Lords are distinctly landowners.   Until
the voice of the people declares in accents
unmistakable and emphatic, that it is
opposed to these laws, nothing can or will
be attempted by the Government.   This is
the mocking answer of the Prime Minister.
Manchester has accepted this challenge, and
proposes to arouse the attention of the
people on the subject.   A committee has
been formed there who are determined to
agitate the question ; to sift the facts ; to
put them before the public ; and thus to

test the national feeling on the subject. It has seemed to them that the time has come when the subject must be dealt with. So long as we had good harvests the land could produce what the population required. But the failure of the harvests has sent up the price of wheat to eighty shillings per quarter. There are many more mouths to feed than there used to be; the area of land under cultivation remains about the same; where are the extra mouths to get bread? How are the empty stomachs to be filled? There are foreign countries which could meet this new demand; but the landowner bars the way, and steps in betwixt the hungry millions and the foreign corn-grower, who would only be too glad to feed them, by the Corn Laws which stand in the way. Sheffield knows what dear bread means in bad times. It means want, hunger, famine!' Here broke out a round of general applause in which the Chartist group joined heartily.

'To keep up the landowners' rents the

people must starve. Further, the manufacturers cannot give the help they willingly would ; because these Corn Laws cripple them too. The upholders of these Laws argue that the manufacturers have a personal interest in the repeal of these Laws. Who denies it ! But it does not follow that their reason is that with cheap bread they could lower wages, as is asserted. If these Laws which restrict commerce were repealed, the manufacturers could pay more wages, and employ more hands; and thus the workmen would benefit as well as their employers. It would be better for every one, all round. I will show you why. We put a tax on imported corn, and thus handicap the foreign corn-grower. He never is sure of what is before him. Even when corn is low he could sell here to a profit if he could get our market price. But as the price falls the duty rises ; and when he has paid the duty there is not enough left to pay him. What is the result ? Instead of growing corn for the English market on the chance of a bad harvest, the foreigner takes to manufactures. They cannot pay for our manufactures with corn, so they manufacture themselves. If they could exchange their corn for our goods, the manufacturer could employ more hands, and pay better wages; while the loaf would be cheaper.' Here came another burst of cheering.

'It is a question—Are the landowners of England to carry the day against all other classes, and all other interests? Have the employers of labour to be crippled, and the employed to hunger, in order to keep up rents? Is it setting class against class to point out how all other classes have to suffer, in order that the landowner may thrive? I think not! The arguments are on our side, and we mean to circulate them thoroughly. We propose to have a newspaper; three lecturers to go about the country; and to spread tracts and pamphlets far and wide; in the firm conviction that a proper knowledge of the facts will guide the nation in its decision. To do this will cost money ; and we propose to provide that money. We say with Cobden : "Let us invest part of our property, in order to save the rest from confiscation." We must part with some in order to save the rest. "For all will go if things do not take a change." He then put formally to the meeting a proposition in accordance with the views expressed in the speech.

The proposition was seconded by another speaker, who said : ' I endorse every word that has been said ; but I should like to point out this fact, that in consequence of cheaper food, the foreign manufacturer can work with smaller wages than we can ; and so is enabled to compete with us. If the price of corn was fairly equal in their country and ours, they could not compete with us. It would be better for them, as well as for us, if they could sell us corn, and with the money buy our goods. But they never know what to look for. The

English corn-merchant can run down prices when corn is coming in freely, and so run up the duty; and then having thus checked the import, run the price up again. Our troubles are aggravated by systematic gambling in corn. We have entered upon bad times; we have had a short harvest; and that, coming upon the top of slack trade, has made food very dear, while there is little money to buy it with; and unless we can get relief by the repeal of the Corn Laws, we must all look out for much privation. I beg to second the motion.' The crowd cheered lustily.

Just at this moment, a tall figure arose from among the Chartist group, mounting a chair that had been brought in readiness; and, in loud stentorian tones, a Chartist speaker proposed an amendment to the proposition. He adduced the usual Chartist arguments in favour of reform, and then proceeded to argue: 'The Corn Laws are bad, we all admit. They are the outcome of class legislation, and intended to protect the interests of the landed party, which furnishes most of our law-makers. But they are not the only bad laws; nor the only laws which need repealing. Why waste time over a part instead of holding together to carry the whole? If we had the Charter, then we could soon get rid of all the bad laws.' Here the group of Chartists cheered loudly. A voice was heard from the other side of the Square: 'Better get a part, than get nothing in trying for too much,' in the lulls of the cheering. This was the essence of the antagonism betwixt the reformers who looked to the Charter to put all right, and the Anti-Corn Law agitator, who aimed at one particular object; and would not be diverted therefrom.

At last, when the noise had abated, another speaker mounted the chair, and inveighed against the 'new movement as a purely selfish action on the part of the manufacturers; and calculated to cause division amidst the ranks of reformers. He condemned it, and seconded the amendment put before the meeting, to the effect that the meeting was in favour of the Charter, and would support the Chartist agitation; and was not in favour of the restricted Anti-Corn Law agitation. The Chartists again cheered; but it became clearer and more apparent than before, that they formed only a decided minority of the meeting; though Sheffield was a stronghold of Chartism.

The amendment was put to the vote, and the president of the meeting counted the hands held up. Plenty from all sides of the Square followed the count; there was no mistake as to the number of hands held up. At first the impression was to the effect that the number was so large it must amount to a majority of those present. But when the original motion was put, the number of hands was at once seen to be greater. The count was carefully made; and it was found that, in reality, there was a majority of two to one in favour of the original motion for attacking the Corn Laws by appeal to public opinion. The Chartists were quite taken by surprise, and could scarcely believe their eyes and ears; but it was impossible to mistake the conclusion. They were dumbfoundered thereat.

The crowd gradually dispersed, and eager conversation ruled everywhere. Mr. Carlyon said to John Wharton:

'What do you say to the result?'

'I am considerably surprised thereat.'

'How has it come about?'

'It is quite clear that there is a great party of free-traders in the country, who do not go the length of the Charter. Also, I fancy, that a section of the reformers would rather try for a distinct and feasible object, like the repeal of the obnoxious Corn Laws, than try for an ideal which has little prospect of attainment.'

'Quite right. Besides, it is more like the English character to strive for an attainable concrete something, than to seek an idea more like a French revolution. I have never supported the Charter; for I could not believe in its ever being carried.'

' I have felt compelled to support it on principle. The principle is right; but the practice may have less to recommend it. These physical force fellows injure it by their appeal to violence. I cannot uphold threats. Still I hold the principle to be right. Like you, I have my doubts as to the possibility of carrying the Charter. This movement has more promise in it,' replied John Wharton.

' Violence will be met by force. The Whigs would like more violence at heart; and then they could put down the whole movement. " Finality John," and Lord Melbourne, and one or two more have pronounced against Reform; and would like to stamp out the movement. But they have not the same objection to the Corn Law repeal. If the distress keeps on increasing, " Finality John " will pretty certainly be ready to try the repeal of the Corn Tax.'

' You think so ? '

'Decidedly. The Conservative party are never likely to espouse the repeal of laws which serve them well; as being more distinctly landowners than the Whigs. The fixed determination to have nothing to do with the Chartists, to enter upon no political subjects except the Corn Laws, and the Corn Laws solely; and their disavowal of anything but peaceful means for the carrying of their end: these two great principles of the Corn Law repealers will embarrass the Government. The arguments they have used against the Chartist movement will scarcely meet the present occasion.'

Such and such-like were the conversations held everywhere. The one given above may serve as a specimen of the views of the more moderate repealers; but more forcible views were expressed by others. The Chartists were highly chagrined by the vote; and vented their rage in furious threats, which the wilder section were not at all unlikely to put into execution. At such a time the prudent counsels of the more moderate party were not likely to be either acceptable or heeded.

'I must say good-bye, Mr. Carlyon. I see a gentleman I must speak to,' said John Wharton, who had caught sight of George Ashworth's lofty figure towering over the crowd.

'Good-bye, Mr. Wharton. I am very glad to have made your acquaintance. I can now say that I have met a landowner at an Anti-Corn Law meeting, when any strong assertion is made in my presence about the attitude of the landowners.'

'Please do not hold me up as a traitor to my class. That would not be pleasant.'

'I understand you,' and the old gentleman nodded kindly, as much as to say—'I shall not hold you up in any unfavourable light'—'I hope we shall meet again. I come to Buxton in the summer months. John Wharton, Esq., Landowner and Corn Law Repealer, near Sheffield. Will that find you if I write to you?'

'I hardly think that will do; though it

might find me. There is my card ; good-
bye.'

John Wharton made his way towards
George Ashworth, and shaking hands cordially, they went off together. The inquiries
after Miss Wharton were necessarily brief ;
but it was welcome news to Ashworth that
Miss Wharton had quite recovered from the
effects of her accident : and he sent a brief
message to her to that effect. He thought
for a moment perhaps she might have sent
a word to him ; but soon he saw that was
out of the question, if it were only for the
reason that she could not know that he was
to be present at the meeting. Both were
full of the meeting, the arguments, the
result of the count, and the petition to be
sent up to Parliament as the outcome of
the meeting, for the repeal of the obnoxious
laws. In five days the petition was sent
off to London, bearing no less than thirteen
thousand signatures.

Such was the response Sheffield gave to
the movement over the moors at Manchester.

CHAPTER VI.

MIXED MOTIVES.

In the good years of ample harvests and thriving trade which preceded the times here spoken of, a bank had been established at Wybrow. The two great promoters of the bank were a Mr. Waddington, a manufacturer; and a Mr. Mortlake, a wealthy corn-merchant. Both had some spare capital which they wished to make remunerative; and they agreed to start a bank. They were very select in their choice of shareholders; and only men of local position were asked to take up scrip-shares. Indeed it was an honour as well as a clear pecuniary advantage to be permitted to join the Wybrow Bank. Squire Wharton had been asked to join in the scheme, but, as he explained before, Mr. Waddington's high-handed behaviour had roused his Wharton touchiness, and he had held aloof; to his loss, as he said. Stephen Oldfield had also been invited to join in the venture, and had gladly taken shares. He had a comfortable property; but he had had to clear off a mortgage, which, together with his keeping up appearances, had prevented his possessing much capital. This, however, was no great difficulty, as the first call was only fifty shillings on the hundred-pound share. So he took five hundred shares; and deposited twelve hundred and fifty pounds; no large sum for him.

The scheme of the promoters was as follows :—They would start with a guaranteed capital of such amount as would secure the confidence of the people around Wybrow. By having local landowners to take shares the utmost certainty was secured as to this confidence. Instead of subscribing all the capital at once, which would be very difficult to raise, and might much of it

lie idle, they adopted the plan of scrip-shares,
the usual one, by which a small deposit only
was paid up at once ; and the rest could be
called upon if required. It is an alluring
prospect, because the small sum paid up is
often not exceeded ; unless, perhaps, by a
second call equal in amount to the first.
Even with this second call Mr. Oldfield
would be getting the advantages of a fifty
thousand pounds investment with an outlay
of two thousand five hundred 'pounds. It
is not the money actually paid up, but the
magic of the guaranteed capital which
draws the profits. With the guarantee in
the form of shareholders of means and
position, the people readily deposited their
money with the bank. The depositors got
two and a half per cent. for their money ;
which was lent out again at five per cent.
The shareholders drew two and a half per
cent., less working expenses, on the money
deposited with them. They did not work
with their own paid up money, but with
the money. deposited at the bank ; the

depositors being safe with the guaranteed capital. By prudence and good management the concern was humanly certain to pay. The Wybrow Bank commanded the confidence of the locality, and soon was a prosperous, thriving concern. Those who had not been invited to take shares, held themselves as aggrieved in being shut out from the golden harvest the harvesters were reaping.

Stephen Oldfield found his shares in the Wybrow Bank a very pleasant addition to his income. Not only did they make housekeeping easy, but the additional income allowed him to indulge in pleasing visions for the future. He had seen how the investment would make Huz his firstborn, and Buz his brother, with any little sisters which Providence might send him when he married, welcome and welcomed. There would be no straitness, no *res angusta domi*. There would be plenty for all; and if more was needed a like venture would procure the desired means. There was scarcely a

sufficient element of risk about the concern
to entitle it to be called a venture. Mr.
Oldfield always treated Messrs. Waddington
and Mortlake with that courtesy all readily
extend to men who have put money into
their pockets—and, what is more, may some
day put greater sums into their pockets.
The country gentleman could treat a manufacturer and a corn-merchant as belonging
to his order under these especial circumstances. Once a year Mr. Oldfield invited
his co-shareholders to dine with him at
Orton Hall. When so met, they regarded
themselves as the benefactors of the district;
and not only did they themselves think so,
but their neighbours shared the opinion
with them. The Wybrow Bank was spoken
of with respect; both by those who deposited
their savings with it, and by those who
borrowed from it. The country folks preferred to keep their spare cash with people
of whom they knew something. Borrowers
were glad to get the money somewhere;
and potential borrowers were civil and

respectful to capitalists to whom they might one day have to apply. The few shareholders were greeted with respect on all hands. Stephen Oldfield certainly enjoyed his position at once as Squire of Orton Hall, and one of the shareholders of the prosperous Wybrow Bank. These shareholders kept themselves familiar with the main proceedings of the bank, and knew what was going on. No sum of any importance was lent out without the subject coming before their notice. They constituted a board of directors, to which the bank-manager had to submit his operations. This was a great matter with depositors, who felt the utmost security in the bank; as they knew that a careful scrutiny was exercised, and no advances made without the requisite security. No borrower must appear without his surety to be bound for him. The Wybrow Bank was inexorable on that head. The general impression abroad was, that this bank made no bad debts. But with a trustworthy surety with him, the borrower was accommodated with the utmost readiness, and politely too withal.

There was no limited liability in the matter; each shareholder was liable to the full extent of his fortune. The depositors could never come to grief. The borrowers knew they were on the right side. It was just this question of unlimited liability which made the success of the bank a matter of paramount interest to the shareholders. It was only in case of a heavy loss that any further call might become necessary; and a heavy loss was not very likely with such men as steered the Wybrow Bank. Mr. Waddington was well known as a prosperous manufacturer, with several good investments. Mr. Mortlake's operations were of some magnitude, and he too was held 'a safe man.' The two other shareholders were men of property, residing on the other side of Wybrow. The private property of these five shareholders was a guarantee which could not be called in question; a trustworthy surety for the bank. When

John Wharton alluded to Stephen Oldfield's having his foot deep in the Wybrow Bank, he referred to this unlimited liability in case things went wrong. Oldfield's estates were worth more than fifty thousand pounds; though that would be a heavy charge on them. But if anything did go seriously wrong, he was liable as long as a penny remained unpaid to the last farthing that he possessed. But the danger was speculative rather than real.

When the bad harvest came, the deposits from the farming element ceased to expand; indeed showed a marked tendency to become stationary. If bad times continued, these balances would shrink; and then farmers would be borrowers rather than depositors. This was recognized, and the bank made its arrangements accordingly. Amongst the rest their inquiry into the validity of a borrower's surety became very searching. The people held this as a proof of the prudence of the management.

As the spring of 1839 wore on, wheat

kept up to that price that foreign corn came in with a very small duty; and without such imports, bread would have been at famine prices. But, though corn was so high, the harvest had been such a poor one the farmers were short of money. Many went to the Wybrow Bank for advances against the spring sowing, and though accompanied by good sureties could not be accommodated. To increase the working capital the prospect of a new call was mooted. This was a grave matter. Five per cent. on money advanced would not allow money well invested to be withdrawn by the bank. To put on a mortgage at four per cent. to lend at five, left one per cent., which would not meet the legal expenses so incurred until several years had passed. If any rumours of the bank being straitened for funds got about, the lessening stream of deposits might disappear, and a drain of withdrawals set in.

' Merit is other people's opinion of you,' said Talleyrand; and advances had been

made to some friends of the two chief pro-
moterson securities which it was found were
not readily negotiable ; and there was a real
pinch. A further call on the shareholders
was unavoidable. They kept the fact to
themselves ; but the money had to be
raised. Mr. Stephen Oldfield had always
been an acute and ready critic of the
actions of others ; but when he came to
have to take action himself, he found it
neither so easy nor so simple as he had
always assumed. It was impossible to
press the persons to whom these advances
had been made. But if it turned out
that the securities, after all, were valueless ?
A cold shiver of anticipation ran down his
back. For the first time he surveyed the
dark side of his connection with the Wybrow
Bank. He did not know what other
schemes the two promoters might be mixed
up with. If anything went wrong with
the bank, Orton Hall might have to go !
The thought was terrible ; for a time it paralyzed him. Instead of the pleasing visions

which the Wybrow Bank had hitherto called up in him, he now saw a distinct if distant danger looming up.

The vulpine element was not wanting in Mr. Oldfield's character, nor did it lie very far below the surface. He was responsible to the last penny of what he possessed— 'stock, lock, and barrel.' There was no mistake about that. It might be well to be prepared for the worst, in case the worst did happen. Various schemes floated through his brain ; even to raising a heavy mortgage upon his estate, and investing it somewhere in some one else's name. But that was a very serious matter. Some other plan than that surely must be feasible. Then came other thoughts ; and among them the remembrance of what Squire Wharton said about the canal-shares which would come to his niece. If she married him, he would give them up ; even if the old settlement was not in existence, the Squire would act as if it was. Edith Wharton now had two aspects for him.

Of course the young lady-reader will be inclined to pour out the vials of her wrath as well as her scorn upon such a caitiff lover ; but if she herself be possessed of a fortune in *esse*, or even in *posse*, she may have occasion to find it, as well as herself, may have attractions even for some very nice and very honourable gentleman. Men do not marry for money, they 'go where money is.' So it will not be fair to the prim little gentleman to judge him too severely.

With these canal shares settled strictly upon herself—it would look well in making the arrangements to be scrupulously careful on this head—their income would break his fall ; if a fall should become imminent. There was still such an income as would keep the wolf from the door,—even if the door should not be so imposing in solid oaken grandeur as the front-door of Orton Hall. Under the influence of the new train of thought which had taken possession of him, Mr. Oldfield began to think seriously about Miss Wharton. They had not seen so much of the Whartons during the spring, he remembered. They had not been fortunate in finding them at home; then the Whartons had not called so frequently. How was it? John Wharton had joined the Anti-Corn Law agitation, and his uncle had been very angry about it. How had he heard this? It must have been at the sessions, or somewhere. It was like John Wharton, a quixotic fellow, who did as he pleased, and did not consult his uncle as he ought to do. But when he became his brother-in law he would be on the old Squire's side, he would find. Yes; but the little gentleman realized—I am not his brother-in-law yet! Then his thoughts went to Miss Wharton, and to the proposal he had made her in the year before. She had not definitely refused him; she had allowed him to call her by her Christian name. In this frame of mind he found himself discounting that permission. To take an arithmetical view of such a permission indicated how utterly the lover had become for the time the man of business. She had not forbidden him from asking her again to become his wife. Then the escape from drowning came upon him so suddenly as to make him start. Yes, by the way, what had become of the gallant preserver ? Had he been heard of lately ? How he would have liked to have stood in his place; then came the corroding thought of his own stature ! It had been a question of inches. Had he been there they only could have perished together. That would not have been a happy ending ! Mr. Oldfield was not in the habit of regarding himself as an object of commiseration on account of his straitened proportions; but now a twinge of envy went through him. Had he been as tall as Mr. Ashworth he could have done the same. But he was not a son of Anak; nor could thought add a cubit to his stature. Had this gigantic fellow got in the way of his prospects ? Edith Wharton was just the girl to hold an exaggerated estimate of the value of the service rendered to her. What was it, after all ? Standing ten minutes in water holding up a lovely girl. That the water was cold and muddy was nothing. But young women had these fancies. Suppose John Wharton liked Ashworth better than himself: what then ? Only that it was another instance of Wharton's bad taste. Still it would favour the other candidate for Miss Wharton's hand. Of course he was a candidate ; no one would disdain that chance. He thought sufficiently highly of Miss Wharton and her attractions to understand his rival's admiring her. Rival, indeed ! Why of course he would be. Had that personage been heard of at Fowrass Grange since the episode on the ice ? An angry burning pang of jealousy shot through him. He would ask Maria.

At lunch he led the conversation up to Fowrass Grange.

'We have not seen much of the Whartons lately,' he remarked in an off-hand way.

' No ; we have not : I wonder how it is ? '
was the reply.

' They have not been at home when we
have called, I think.'

' No ; nor have they found us at home,
I remember. It is odd.'

' I wonder how they are. Have you
heard anything of them, Maria, lately ? '

' No ; I only heard some one say that John
Wharton seemed to be making a great
friend of the man who saved his sister's
life. They are both Radicals.'

' Was that all ? ' he inquired, with a distinct emphasis in the tone. His sister at once
surmised what was in her brother's mind.

' He seems to have been at the Grange
several times,' was the guarded answer.

Mr. Oldfield had a curious and singular
practice. He detested flies, and was in the
habit of dropping coins upon them. He
had become exceedingly expert from practice ; and noting the exact position of a fly
upon the table would calculate its place, and
drop a coin upon the unsuspecting insect

with great, indeed almost unerring, precision.
He seemed suddenly to become conscious
that there were several of these winged
and segmented intruders upon the table.
Taking a sovereign from his purse he proceeded to exercise his skill upon the unfortunate *dipteræ;* and soon several motionless
black objects testified to his expertness
and adroitness. His sister did not like the
practice, but she kept her opinion to herself. She saw her brother was absorbed
in thought by the *abandon* with which he
gave himself to his repulsive sport : yet it
was evident that it was not the *muscidæ*
who were the objects of his absorption.
After the remaining flies had seemed to
become conscious of the danger veritably
overhanging them, and maintained a safe
distance,—an intellectual process which Mr.
Romanes would maintain is not beyond
their powers, he replaced the coin in his
purse. After a little more thought he
remarked :

'Maria, I think it desirable to bring

matters to a final issue betwixt myself and Miss Wharton. She must know her mind by now.' His sister listened in amazement: she had no idea of the thoughts which had that morning occupied and exercised her brother's mind.

Within a week or so Mr. Oldfield had carried out his purpose. It fell out in this way. He met Miss Wharton coming down the lawn from Gaythorne Hall. Her tall, erect figure came suddenly upon him from behind a curve in the evergreens. Taken suddenly, he raised his hat, greeted her, and asked if he might turn back with her. The permission was granted, though it could not be said in very encouraging accents. After some commonplaces he entered upon the particular topic.

'You remember our interview some months ago, Edith—' here the girl winced slightly. He noted the movement, slight as it was, and went on: 'It was then you accorded to me the privilege of calling you by your Christian name; a great privilege

I regard it. I then told you the state of
my feelings towards you ; and though you
would not yield to my persuasions at that
time, you gave me permission to address
you again—at some future time—on the
subject.'

'That is so,' was the curt unencouraging
reply. It was quite clear from the manner
of each that their attitude was distinctly
different from what it was on the first
occasion. There seemed less of passionate
affection in the suitor's speech ; less of
sympathy on the part of the lady. Altogether there was a stiffness—a mannerism
in each, which boded no good to the suit.

'After further examination of my feelings I find them unaltered. I find my love
for you, Edith, not only undiminished, but
strengthened, by the lapse of time.' This
was not very loving, and yet the little
man was doing his best. ' Allow me,' he
said, opening the gate for them. Miss
Wharton instinctively compared the little
piece of formality with another man she

knew; the comparison was not to the advantage of her companion. Cupid might have been seen,—if the natural eye could have seen him, unbending his bow, and fastening up his quiver. 'I have hoped, indeed I have, Edith,' he said in a more eager tone, 'that you would turn a more complaisant ear to my pleading than you did before. I have hoped that my love would be returned this time. Have you an answer for me?' He looked at her beseechingly.

'When I gave you permission to address me again, I held out no hope to you that my decision would be other than as before. I too have examined my feelings towards you; and I cannot find any change in them.'

'Do not say so. Do not tell me that. I cannot believe you, Edith!'

'I am sorry if you cannot believe me. I trust your disbelief will not entail our entering upon this subject again, Mr. Oldfield.'

'I cannot think you mean what you say. You are saying so to try me : to test me : to see if my love for you is strong enough to bear repeated rebuffs.'

'I am deeply sorry if you will persist in regarding my answer in that light. I see no prospect of any change in my feelings. Why do you persist in pursuing a course which is so painful to both of us?' This indicated a distinct departure from her former attitude; then she seemed willing to do all she could to spare him pain : now she seemed less tender, less considerate— even aggressive.

'Because I cannot help it. When a man loves a woman heart and soul, he cannot believe she will never return his love,—if he be patient.'

'I am afraid in this case, Mr. Oldfield, the patience will not prevail.' A host of suspicions swept through his mind like a hurricane; why should she be thus certain that time would work no change? As he looked at the beautiful girl, his sense of loss was intensified. For the moment the lower motives of his action were completely in abeyance—out of sight entirely. His lover's wish to possess the beauteous girl was entirely in the ascendant; and a bitterness like the bitterness of death seized upon him. In his agony he continued:

'When I spoke to you before, in answer to my question, you told me that your feelings were not engaged elsewhere; can you say so now?'

'*In veritate victoria*' is the Wharton motto. Miss Wharton was in this respect a Wharton, intensified by her Marston blood. She flushed, and was silent.

'You cannot say so now; I see it!' Here his voice changed with his feelings. 'You have given your heart to another. You have played fast and loose with me. Coquette! I never thought to call you so.'

Miss Wharton was an honest, sincere, truthful girl, and this taunt stung her. She was not sufficiently experienced in proposals to be able to soothe the bruised mind of an unsuccessful suitor, as one well versed in the art.

'I do not know by what right you address me in this way, Mr. Oldfield. We have been old friends—close friends; and when you offered me your hand before, I declined it. If I gave you permission to address me again, I told you to look for no change in my feelings. I now tell you that such change has not come over me. I decline your offer finally. I request you never to address me again on the subject.' It was evident Miss Wharton was stung by the reproach flung at her. 'And another thing I must request of you: and that is, that you do not address me by my Christian name. To permit that would be to allow an unwarranted relation between us to deceive others; to put us, or rather keep us, in a false position' Every word was like the torture of the Red Indian, felt, and felt distinctly. Amidst his general sense of suffering every touch was discerned. Over all was a sense of humiliation. He had offered Miss Wharton his hand, and this time it had been spurned. Yet what was to be done? Social propriety is a great refuge in time of trouble. It was felt so now. Mr. Oldfield raised his hat.

'Miss Wharton, your wishes shall be attended to. I have the honour to wish you good morning,' was the brief speech which passed his lips; but his heart was burning within him.

Each turned to leave the scene,—each absorbed in thought. Edith Wharton felt a sense of relief at having cut for ever the ties betwixt Stephen Oldfield and herself; ties which had begun to gall her. Her uncle would be wroth, she knew. Her brother would not grieve. And some one else! What difference would this make betwixt George Ashworth and herself? Here she found her mind wandering into the regions of the unknown.

Stephen Oldfield raged inwardly. He cursed his own precipitation in bringing up his suit again so soon, instead of letting time work for him. ‘But,’ said reason, ‘has time been working for you lately? It appears not! Before, her feelings were not otherwise engaged: now it seems they are. Your chance has been sliding away for some time. Inevitably too. It was as well to put yourself out of suspense.’ There was a crumb of comfort to be got out of that. Then came the business aspect. How about the possible break-down of the Wybrow bank? Where are the canal-shares which were to have broken the fall? Gone like last winter’s snows; as little to return. As these thoughts crossed his mind, some imp, riding on the gentle breeze, hissed ‘Failed’ into his ear.

‘Failed!’ Yes, he had failed in his courtship. And failure seemed to spread itself over the future from the horizon to the zenith; like a black thunder-cloud coming up fast on a summer’s day. He felt a grim foreboding that this was the commencement of disaster.

CHAPTER VII.

A DINNER-PARTY.

THIS final rejection of Mr. Oldfield led
to certain other incidents ; and before long
it was known that Miss Wharton was
engaged to be married to her preserver,
Mr. Ashworth. Under the circumstances,
that gentleman did not feel himself called
upon to consult the Squire in the matter;
and when John Wharton informed his
uncle of the fact, it is needless to say the
Squire was far from overjoyed.

'She is of age, and of course can please
herself. Girls generally will! But I did
think Edie would have had some consideration for her old uncle. I suppose
Ashworth asked you ?'

'He did : and I gave him my consent to
propose to her cheerfully enough.'

'I dare say you did. He would be glad enough of that. I suppose my consent was unnecessary.' Then after a pause, during which the old Squire seemed to be fanning his wrath, he continued:

'I don't approve of the man; and I will not hand over the canal-shares, as I offered to do if she accepted Oldfield. I can please myself, and I will too.'

'You are quite entitled to do that, uncle.'

'Yes; and I will too. In the absence of the original settlement, I can dispose of the shares as I like. I will not withdraw the allowance I make Edie. I will not show ill-temper at my own niece; but she might have consulted me!'

'It is very good of you to promise to continue the allowance. They will have to practise some economy.'

'That I dare say. If she would have taken Oldfield, she could have lived like a Wharton. As she makes her bed, so she must lie. I will continue the allowance; but I will promise nothing about the whole stock. That is mine; and I will do as I like with it.'

John Wharton saw his uncle was nettled at the engagement: and suspected that his sister's reason for not consulting him on the subject was, that she had her own reasons for abstaining from so doing; probably believing that he would withhold his consent. If she had made up her mind to accept George Ashworth, it was just as well not to offend her uncle by asking him about it; and then acting contrary to his wishes. So he tried to keep the peace as much as possible.

' I think she acted deliberately in refusing Oldfield.'

' Very likely. And her liking for this other fellow had a good deal to do with it, I'll be bound. If he had not got in the way, all would have been well. I wish you both had been up here that afternoon when the ice gave way. I saw what would happen; but I did not think Edie would have acted independently of her uncle in a

matter so important as this. I am grieved
—very grieved about it.'

That the old Squire was greatly hurt
was at once obvious and intelligible. But
as it is neither a legal requirement nor a
customary practice for girls to marry only
those of whom their relatives approve,
in so acting Edith Wharton only did what
is common enough. The old Squire was a
trifle unreasonable in his complaint; and yet
one must sympathize with him. When his
niece went to see him the next day, his
ill-humour had not vanished.

'And so you are engaged to be married,
Edie? And never let your old uncle
know about it! I did not expect that!'

'Dear uncle, I did not wish to wound
you. I knew you did not like George
Ashworth. I owe him my life. And I
have promised him my hand. I cannot
take back my pledged word; as a Wharton.'

'No; you cannot. But I wish you had
not given your word. Come, give your old
uncle a kiss. I wish it had been some one

else. My congratulations are not very warm, I fear.' The matter was got over; but the old Squire was far from satisfied about it all the same. As he proposed to continue the yearly allowance, he felt himself entitled to make all inquiries into Ashworth's family, his antecedents, and his prospects. Mr. Chadwick, his man of business, gained all the desired particulars. There was nothing wrong; yet the Squire did not profess to be pleased with the match.

'It is scarcely befitting a Wharton,' he would conclude, adding: 'I wish the fellow had not been one of those radical-reforming Chartists. One cannot give up one's views as well as one's niece. I suppose I must learn to put up with him.'

The spring went on, and was very cold and dry. The price of wheat had fallen to seventy shillings a quarter, making the duty according to the sliding-scale over ten shillings a quarter. The Anti-Corn Law agitation was going on briskly. The rival movement of the Chartists had been embarrassed by some want of union in their ranks. The delegate representing Sheffield had resigned his post in consequence thereof.

The landowners in turn had been taking steps for the protection of their own interests ; and Squire Wharton had determined to give a dinner-party, and then the position of affairs could be thoroughly discussed. It came off about the end of May.

It was not a large gathering. There were present : Canon Wordsworth, Squire Oldfield, Mr. Pryor, John Wharton ; two other local landowners and magistrates, Messrs Moorhouse and Broadhurst ; and a clergyman, Mr. Ripley, of Tory instincts and sluggish liver. A small, comfortable dinner-party, not too numerous for the conversation to become divided.

'It has been a fine dry spring for farming operations,' was the remark of the Canon, —who took a great interest in mundane matters, as they sat down at the table.

'It has kept dry rather too long. I am

afraid we must make up our minds to a short hay-crop. "Plenty of rain in May, and plenty of corn and hay," is the old adage. I am afraid straw will be short unless the weather alters,' rejoined Mr. Moorhouse.

'It does not matter so much about the straw if the corn in the ear is there. Drought never brought dearth in England, you know,' said Mr. Broadhurst.

'We seem to have an adage to apply whichever way things turn,' observed Mr. Oldfield.

'Yes. It is curious,' remarked the little Tory clergyman. 'But it brings comfort with it. I hope there will be a better harvest than there was last year.'

'Why? Is the man who farms your glebe behind with his rent, Ripley?'

A slight laugh went round the table, as Ripley was given to complaining.

'No. But he may be if there is another short harvest; whether it be from a scanty yield, or bad weather. It does not matter.'

'You are only like the rest of us, Ripley.

We must share and share alike, you know,' said Mr. Pryor.

'You can have your share and mine too of bad times,' was the retort; which created some amusement, none enjoying it more than the provoker.

'It is very generous of you, I am sure, Ripley,' was the genial answer.

'Do you think we will have another bad yield?' asked Mr. Oldfield of the company at large. 'No, thank you, Bulman, that is a beautiful trout, but it is too much. You have helped me too liberally, Mr. Wharton. It is a pity to cut it; let me have a smaller fish, please.'

'I think you might manage a trout like that, if you tried hard. But, however, I'll accommodate you.'

'Where did you kill these trout, Jack?'

'In the Don.'

'I suppose the May-fly is on the water now,' asked the Canon.

'It has just come on; the cold dry

season has kept it back. It is a bad fishing season.'

'I suppose the poachers have cleared out the streams pretty well,' remarked Mr. Broadhurst. 'They would be sure to do that—these Chartist fellows Nothing would please them better than robbing a trout-stream.

'And so getting a slap at their oppressors, the landowners,' said John Wharton.

'If they did nothing more than rob the trout-streams, we need not mind. But they are plotting more objectionable measures by far. I am afraid we will have some trouble before long; especially if corn is dear next winter.'

'They are a bad set in Sheffield, I fear, remarked the host. 'They are always ready for some violence there; but the yeomanry will keep them in check.'

'Yes. The yeomanry can be thoroughly relied upon. They know their own interests, and can be depended upon. Though I do not give much credence to the talk about the soldiers sympathizing with the people,' was the Canon's opinion.

'I sincerely trust there may be no occasion to need the services of either,' said the Rector. 'It is hard to be poor.'

'Yes: that it is,' put in Mr. Ripley, in a tone which left no question about his views.

'Even with a comfortable roof over your head, and a sufficiency of food,' John Wharton observed. 'And therefore a great deal harder for those who have neither.'

'Come now. Let us have none of your reforming views at your uncle's table, John,' the Canon said good-naturedly. 'You may air them elsewhere. Unless you are going to abandon them! I think, Wharton, we should get him on the commission of the peace; that would secure him.'

'I don't know; he's a headstrong fellow.'

'Do you mean he has a strong head?' asked the Rector. 'If it were not for his modesty I should be apt to give him a certificate of character in that respect.'

'It is very kind, but I think we will dispense with your friendly offer for the present;' said the host.

'What are your Anti-Corn Law friends going to do, John?' pursued the Canon.

'Get the Corn Laws repealed if they can!'

'I suppose so. What are they doing?'

'They have got out a newspaper of their own, with some rather appropriate texts on it. Have you seen it?' asked Mr. Moorhouse.

'Yes. I think them blasphemous the way they are used,' said Mr. Ripley.

'No; I don't think you can call them more than irreverent,' was Mr. Pryor's comment.

'What are they?' asked the Canon.

'One is—"The bread of the needy is his life; he that depriveth him thereof is a man of blood!" It is to the point anyhow,' explained Mr. Pryor.

'Then we assembled here are mostly men of blood in the eyes of the needy ! Complimentary, to say the least of it. Anything more ?'

'The other is—" He that withholdeth corn, the people shall curse him." I wonder what Mortlake would say to that ! He is holding for a rise,' the Rector continued.

'These operations of the corn-merchants enrage the people. They can always keep corn up above a fair market price,' said John Wharton.

Mr. Oldfield felt it became him to uphold the character of a shareholder in the Wybrow Bank, so he explained :

'Mortlake is no worse than the other corn-merchants ; only he is bolder.'

'And no better,' replied the Rector. 'I should not be at all surprised to find his house sacked by the mob, or fired, some of these days. There are some rough fellows about Barnsley.'

'Then they must be kept in order,' said the Canon, in authoritative tones, feeling

like a magistrate. 'We cannot permit
lawlessness and riot. They may threaten
to burn my house; but that will not frighten
me.'

'They are holding a number of meetings
at Sheffield and elsewhere. It is a good
thing those torchlight gatherings were put
down. But I fear we will have trouble,
when the shorter days come. I feel a little
anxiety,' remarked Mr. Broadhurst.

'There is a mutinous spirit abroad, I
fear,' said the Canon. 'What do you think
of the complications in Canada, Wharton?
You know the colony well. What do you
say about Lord Durham's proposal?'

'It is a bold scheme, but I do not think
it can be carried out; and if it were there
would always be discontent among some.
They are too near the States for peace.
The Canadians are loyal in their way; but
it is only a threat on the part of their
neighbours to annex them which brings it
to a white heat. Then they are loyal
enough. They stood well by the royal

troops in the old days; and would again, I quite believe. The insurrection was far from general.'

'Durham seems quite to take the view that the people are right in demanding control over their own affairs; that is, their internal affairs, as compared to imperial affairs,' said Mr. Ripley; 'but I do not hold with him.'

'It is this confounded reforming spirit that is abroad. The people must know better than their rulers! It was well the insurrection was put down so soon.'

'The United States behaved well in the matter. If they had supported the insurgents Toronto might have fallen,' said Mr. Pryor.

'They could not act otherwise without giving occasion for war, that I see,' Mr. Oldfield put in.

'What caused the outbreak?' asked Mr. Moorhouse. 'I forget now.' It was more probable he never knew; but no one was rude enough to suggest such a correction, of course.

'They would not pay the charges of the Civil Government, which had got into arrears, unless they had free elections and legislators chosen by themselves. The Home Government would not yield all their demands, and civil war broke out. The loyalist settlers rallied to the Government, and the insurgents were suppressed,' explained their host.

'Lord Durham thinks that a federation of the several provinces into a dominion with complete internal control over themselves, desirable. In fact, admits their claims,' said the Canon. 'It seems a great matter.'

'Lord Durham is only acting as one might expect. He was the real soul of the Reform party. Without him his father-in-law Grey would never have engaged in the struggle,' John Wharton remarked.

'He was the man to send out, according to the tenets of the Whig Government; only it is not certain that his recommendations will be accepted. What then?' inquired the Rector of Brigstone.

'It does not seem likely that he can hold on if his own party will not adopt his scheme. It will be rather hard on him if they don't,' was the Canon's opinion.

'Then let something else be done. But what has that something to be?' asked Mr. Moorhouse in a vague way.

'Put them down and leave them,' suggested Mr. Ripley.

'But Brougham thinks they were put down only too thoroughly.'

'Do you think he was right, Pryor?'

'Well, to condemn men without a trial is scarcely the English idea of justice.'

'It may not be law, but it is justice; if you mean being right served,' the Squire remarked.

'The Government may not stay in office long,' put in Mr. Moorhouse.

'I think Peel will succeed next time in forming a Ministry. It was a queer thing about the Bed-chamber question.'

'But he was right,' broke in Mr. Ripley.

'Well; but Lady Sunderland and Lady Rialton continued in the bed-chamber of Queen Anne, after their husbands had been dismissed from office,' put in John Wharton.

'The precedent scarcely applies here. Queen Anne was a woman of mature years. Our present Queen is but a girl,' explained the Canon.

'There was nothing said about the conduct of the ladies, I think. It was a mere matter of principle with Peel?'

'You are right there, Pryor. But it was a harsh proceeding to insist upon her giving up her private friends,' said John Wharton.

'The Queen ought to yield on matters of that kind,' observed Mr. Moorhouse, who belonged to the extreme wing of the Tories; at that time by no means loyal, and dreadfully jealous of Lord Melbourne's influence with the Queen. 'It is not proper for the Queen to take sides in politics.

'But has she taken a side?' broke in the Squire hotly. 'She had a right to keep trusted friends around her ; even if they were Whigs.'

'I think the point might very well have been yielded,' interposed the Canon, in the interests of harmony. 'However, if Peel gets into power at the next general election it will matter little.'

Here the table was cleared, and as a consequence the conversation was interrupted. The cloth was removed, and the decanters were placed before the host. There were port and sherry, of course, and some claret. The Canon observed:

'You still keep to the claret, Wharton. I thought it had almost entirely gone out. Port is the wine for a Yorkshireman !'

' So I think. But nephew Jack does not care about it. He has learned to drink claret in his visits to the continent. He will scarcely touch port.'

' Perhaps he will take to it in time ?'

'I wish I saw some signs of it. I have a good stock of '20 port in the cellar ; and I have laid down some '34. It is the best

vintage since '20 ; though '28 was not a bad wine. It will take me some years to get through it. And you know I would not like to think of it being wasted. This troublesome gout compels me to be careful.'
The old Squire spoke as he felt ; that this really was a minor trial in life. The Canon thoroughly sympathized with him : and a mutual respect for port wine is a bond of union no water-drinker can ever comprehend. So he remarked :

'Well, if he does not drink it himself, he will always have a glass of good port for his friends. Gaythorne Hall must never be without a glass of good port.'

Here the Canon looked into space ; as if he was trying to conjecture such a contingency, and failing to realize it.

'I hope it may be a long time before I am consulted in the matter. I am sure uncle wears well ; don't you think so ?'

'Very prettily said, for an heir-at-law. He is a good Wharton, Squire, for all he is tinctured with these new-fangled notions.'

'Yes; it is a pity. But I hope he will never forget himself so far as to let the stock of port run low. I could not like to think of that.' Radicalism might possibly be overlooked; but that port should be neglected was inconceivable!

'I hope there will always be some for me when I call,' went on the Canon.

To love port wine, and to be a judge of it; and, further, to be rather proud thereof, was neither sin nor weakness, at that day, in an ecclesiastic.

'I hope so too,' was the heir's rejoinder.

The other gentlemen had been discussing the proposed postal changes, and had not quite agreed in their views; Mr. Moorhouse feeling quite sure that a penny stamp would never cover the expense, and that the Post-Office must be a loser by the change. The Rector of Brigstone argued in favour of it.

'It will be a great boon to the poor. The rich can write freely: the rich without cost; but the poor, especially in these hard times, are precluded from communicating with each other : that is, unless they resort to some manœuvre. A while ago I was going round the parish, when I saw the postman call at a cottage, and hand a letter to the woman occupying it. After looking at it awhile carefully, she shook her head and handed it back. "I cannot afford the money," was her reason. I was just coming out of the next cottage, and, hearing this, I inquired into the circumstances ; thinking I might pay the postage of it for her if it was of importance. "No thank you, sir," she said. "It is from my brother ; he is a soldier in Ireland. There is nothing in the letter. We agreed to write to each other ; and if there was anything in the letter there was to be a cross in the top right-hand corner, and then the postage was to be paid. He is all right ; there was no cross." You see, the Post-Office loses on a number of letters.'

'It was a very clever dodge,' remarked Mr. Ripley, who had found letter-writing a luxury beyond his means ; except when he

could get some franks, which was not
often.

'It is a pity that the people should be
reduced to such subterfuges,' continued the
Rector.

'Would you be in favour of doing away
with franking? Don't you think it ought
to have been retained? A member of
Parliament has to write lots of letters as a
member; surely the postage of these should
not come out of his own pocket?' remarked
Mr. Broadhurst.

'It would be a lesser evil than the old
one of taxing the people and letting off the
peers,' was the Rector's reply.

'You are always with the people,' Mr.
Oldfield remarked, in a tone as if Mr. Pryor
was to side with his own class always, as he
did himself.

'Won't you take some wine?' asked their
host; and all settled down to their wine after
dinner in a grave, serious, business-like manner,—befitting the solemnity of the occasion.

The conversation wandered backwards

and forwards, now to national topics, now
to local affairs, and brought out considerable
diversity of opinions; it being very clear
from the opinions expressed to which side
of the political parties the speaker leaned.
It was a point of honour to retain family
opinions as to politics at that time : and
each man swore by his own political organ.
Of course 'The Sheffield Independent' was
perused by all of them on account of its
local interest, but without reference to its
views; but otherwise the rule held good.
The good dinner and the port had loosened
the tongue of each. Then cigars went
round; for the Squire had never laid aside
his practices as a soldier entirely; but only
John Wharton and Mr. Broadhurst availed
themselves of the opportunity.

The conversation wandered once more to
Canada, and to the attack on the big house
at St. Denis, where the insurgents beat off
the attack.

'It was a foolish thing not to wait for
the guns to come up : but they despised

the insurgents, that was the mistake. There
was some warm work with the Americans,
many of whom were rather backwoodsmen
than regular soldiers,—in the war on the
lakes. Some of the men who had served
under the Duke admitted that. At Niagara
Falls we had a very brisk encounter. We
were lying below the Falls when the Americans came on in full feather about the
Chippewa affair. It was in 1814 ; a lovely
July evening after sunset ; the sky was
beautifully clear, and the moon on the
wane. We were so near the cataract that
it could be heard above the roar of battle.
There was some cover on our left wing, and
the enemy took advantage of it to make a
flank movement. Nothing but seasoned
troops could have stood such an attack.
As it was, the enemy gained the field for a
time ; but we recovered it after the surprise
was over. It was a near thing though.
While Jessop was taking us in flank on the
Queenstown road under shelter of the cover,
another man was creeping up in front under

the slope until he was near enough the battery to shoot down the gunners. They are good shots, these backwoodsmen, and picked them off just at the nick of time: it was well planned. They gained the guns, and I thought the day would go against us. But we quickly rallied from the surprise, and turned on them. They could not stand the charge when it came to hand-to-hand work. We drove them off, and recaptured all the guns but one; they managed to get it away. They could fight as well as we could, and they were up to a lot of clever moves; but when we got near with the bayonet they did not care so much about it. They claimed the day; but we had a better right to it. I will never forget looking up the wounded while the roar of the Falls nearly deafened us. It warms up an old soldier's blood to think of those days.'

The old Squire paused as Bulman came in with the coffee.

'Ah, do you remember Niagara Falls—
the fight I mean, Bulman?'

'I am not likely to forget it, sir,' was the
brief, soldier-like answer.

'You were behind looking after my traps
when the men fell back; and was afraid I
was killed.'

'I was, sir. I thought you were.'

Master and man alike remembered the
fray.

After some further conversation the
guests took their departure; and Gaythorne
Hall relapsed into its wonted quiet.

CHAPTER VIII.

OVER THE MOORS.

When John Wharton left Mr. Carlyon after the Sheffield meeting in January, it was arranged that the latter would inform him when he had come to take up his summer residence at Buxton. A letter had been received giving John Wharton a cordial invitation to visit him there. Peak Cottage could provide entertainment for man and beast, if he would ride over and stay a few days. The invitation was readily accepted; as John Wharton was desirous of resuming his acquaintance with the handsome old gentleman, with whom he found himself in such accord. It was decided that the visit should come off in the latter part of July. He had not left his sister for so long a time, since the death of their mother; and was anxious lest she should be lonely in his absence.

'Do not think of me, John. You are such a stay-at-home bird; you never get away. I shall do very well, I can assure you. I am anxious to know what the Carlyons are like. My curiosity is aroused.'

Edith Wharton had given herself more completely to house-keeping matters since her engagement. 'We are going to be poor people, who practise economy. We must make everything go the furthest. So I must start, and learn to be economical. Not that we are very extravagant in our house-keeping, Jack. Are we?'

'Wickedly wasteful, Edie. Our way of going on is simply reprehensible. I think I shall have to ask Mr. Pryor to rebuke us from the pulpit, as an example to our neighbours of what should not be. What do you say to that?'

'Go away, and don't talk such nonsense.'

'Go away; that is precisely what I am going to do! I suppose in my absence you will practise economy with a vengeance, and half-starve yourself. I am afraid Ashworth will not be at hand, to see to your goings-on.'

'And if he was, I do not think he would come here in your absence. We are not so head-and-ears in love that we forget what is proper. I wonder if you will see any one you will fancy. If you are left alone you will need a woman's care; that is my belief.'

'That is an aspect of my visit that has not struck me before.'

'That is very likely. The stupendous male intellect soars above these little matters of every-day life; which a woman never overlooks. You are going to meet your fate, as the people here put it; see if you don't?'

'I will try to bear the subject in mind, Edie. You won't be lonely?'

'No, thank you, brother mine, I shall

manage very well. Unless the Chartists come out. But they will not attack Fowrass Grange. That is certain enough. One useful outcome of your radicalism anyhow!'

So one fine morning early, while the larks were soaring and singing, John Wharton rode out of the gate, and went slowly westward, up the hill-side to the moors; having Featherbed Moss on his left. It was a lovely morning, with the remains of the mist rising as the sun's rays dissolved it. The road swept upwards amidst purple heather and pale green bracken, with deeper-shaded mosses on the black peaty soil. The walls were of freestone, bounding the road, for thorn fences do not thrive on the summits of the back-bone of England. Then, here and there, were little white-washed farm-houses with their tiny farm-buildings; the characteristic moorland farm-steads. The short, firm-leaved bilberry lined the road-sides; while now and again a small stunted birch could be seen.

Out of the heather sprang at intervals the lusty grouse, with sharp whirr of wings, and short sharp cry. The rider held a loose rein, and Hawk cast his head about freely with a repeated snort; an invitation to his rider to tighten his rein, and let him increase his speed. But his rider seemed too absorbed; or in no mood to push his horse up the rising ground. 'Patience, Hawk, it is very pleasant. Don't be in a hurry; you shall go faster after a while.' The horse seemed to catch the gist of the speech sufficiently to realize that his rider was not inclined to get on faster. Having made the ascent, his rider gathered up the reins and trotted over the summit. The horse enjoyed the more rapid pace, and unwillingly obeyed the rein, when the road began to slope.

'It is a pity to miss this view, Hawk,' said the rider as he drew up.

It was a fine sight indeed. From the purple-clad moors he looked away over a pleasant agricultural district at his feet.

There were pastures with cattle and sheep, lazily grazing as if the edge of their morning appetite was gone. Patches of corn, green, but short with the dry weather, were scattered about; while fields of pale green dotted with hay-cocks were numerous. Beyond this belt were high chimneys, and masses of houses pretty plentifully strewn about; for the district is one of the most populous of the cotton areas.

'These crowded towns are very sensitive to the price of bread,' was the thought that came up in his mind. 'Coal not far away, a handy seaboard, and a prolific population to fill those mills with lissom-handed workers; this district is admirably suited to be the cotton-factory of the world. I wonder what determined these weaving industries in rooting themselves along these hill-sides. It must have been the water-power. There is a plenteous rainfall on these hills, and tumbling rivulets adapted to water-wheels; with ravines admitting of being readily dammed. That must have had a deal to do with it. The facilities for water-power must be the solution of the problem. It is the same case with the west-land clothiers clustered round the Mendip Hills. And now steam is enabling the mill-owners to push into the plain, overspreading it by degrees. How different is it all from the old days! When black forests ran into bogs and morasses. When the ground I now stand on was the haunt of the wolf, the wild boar, the stag, and even the wild ox itself. The badger found a shelter in the crevices of the rocks; while the eagle built on the crags. Perhaps even the beaver was not altogether extinct. When here and there could be seen a cleared space with the old Saxon village in its centre surrounded by its protective trees; the huts of the ceorls encircling the Ætheling's Grange in its cluster of sycamores, or willows, peopled by rooks. When their population increased, it was but clearing another patch of wood, or taking in a plot from the pasture around.

The problem was a simple one at that day. Then as the country became settled and cleared, enterprising men went out and built here a house and there a house, till the country became studded with isolated farm-houses. There was no pressure on our producing powers then. Indeed at one time corn was exported ; notably when Spain had a sharp pinch in the time of Philip, before the Armada time. But those tall chimneys, and the industrial hordes around them, have turned the scale. If they grow, and the land cannot wax, then bread must be got somehow ; and those abominable Corn Laws stand in the way.' Here his thoughts went away from the scene to Mr. Carlyon, and what they should talk about.

Hawk, relieved by his trot, stepped steadily down the slope, and the scene gradually drew in as horse and rider made the descent.

Here and there were clumps of bramble, then a tuft or two of the prickly shield-fern ; after that a patch of yellow gorse.

The road wound round the base of the hill, and then turned south to Glossop. It was a new country for John Wharton; so he decided to put Hawk up for an hour or two, and have a look about the place. He saw an old coaching inn, and dismounted. Handing his reins to an ostler, he turned into the hostelry, and was struck with the change in the speech of the people. He understood it perfectly; though the pronunciation of many words was considerably different from that of Hallamshire. This marked alteration in the speech on crossing a mountain-ridge is commonly met with in the north of England. Up to Orton in Westmoreland, the speech is that of Lancashire; beyond its Scar it is that of Cumberland. The talk ran on the doings of the Chartists; the course taken by the Anti-Corn Law agitators; the opinions of Lord John Russell inclining to the repeal of the Laws, or at least to a fixed duty to enable the foreign grower to know what he was doing; on the slackness of trade;

the prospects of the hay-crop ; and local matters. Then he sauntered through the town, inspected the churchyard, noted the prevalence of local names on the headstones ; and conducted himself like any other intelligent person in a new locality. Then he had some light refreshment, and mounting Hawk, continued his journey southwards.

He rode away until the Derbyshire hills loomed up on his left. Little rivulets came tumbling down from the hills with water as clear as crystal. The hedgerows were thick and luxuriant; consisting largely of tall hazels, destitute of the sign of a nut, interspersed with blackthorn. Here and there in a sheltered nook, under the hedge, were tufts of the broad-leaved harts-tongue, and, scattered about, a wake-robin or two; further on there were clumps of the shield-fern, no longer the hardy prickly variety of the higher ground, but the ordinary variety, or again of the buckler-fern. The bracken had gone. Then after a turn in the road

came hazels of less luxuriant growth, with
plentiful clusters of nuts ; promising grand
field-days for the youngsters of the neighbourhood. Soon he saw ahead of him an
old building of mediæval origin ; indeed
what once had been a moated grange. But
the moat had disappeared, though the old
high solid walls still remained unshaken.
Behind them a stout resistance could have
been made ; and possibly enough had been
made in the old days of King and Common-
wealth. On the left a park with many old
Scotch firs sloped up towards the hills, at
no great distance. The park-walls also
were high and stout. The road crossing
the stream ran betwixt the park-wall and
the outer walls of the grange ; dark, wet,
and dank were these walls, and the road.
The whole place had been built with strict
regard to warlike purposes, and barred the
highway very effectually. The old walls
were covered with a tiny moss, while their
tops were fringed with the polypody. In
a corner could be seen the unwholesome-

looking hemlock with its deep-green leaves, and its smooth stems spotted with livid markings. On the right the road opened and showed a railed front, a badly-kept lawn, and an old house with wings, built of freestone ; but overspread with lichen till it looked grey and venerable. Opposite was a large gate opening into the park ; and, beyond it, a clear pebbly stream, with no bridge, but a row of stepping-stones, regular and evidently well-trodden. Then came the high, damp walls again, and after that a gate across the road. Beyond this lay a village with a large green ; the sward of which was better kept by the geese pasturing on it, than the lawn of the mansion. Numerous geese were grazing about, while ducks were plentiful in the stream. Round some of the houses were several fowls, mainly game fowls with their lordly Sultans, black-reds, and duck-wings. ' A little surreptitious cock-fighting goes on here evidently, was the thought which passed through the traveller's mind. Conspicuous was the

Harrow Inn; and close to it a saw and grist mill on the stream. Along the left of the village ran the mill-race; while the village green was cut up by the overflowing streams. A quiet scene it was, for all were out in the hay-fields. A little further on stood the Blue Bell without a sign of life in it. After that was the mill-dam, and a slight distance beyond a bridge spanning the stream. It too was grey with lichen; while little tufts of the tiny bladder-fern grew out of the crevices between the stones. A heavy, substantial, solid bridge it was, intended to withstand the torrent when swollen by winter rains. But the stream was dwarfed by the dry summer; and the big boulders in its bed were yellow and dry. Looking over the ledge of the bridge he spied a black trout, wary from experience, making for a safe retreat beneath a massive stone. A less safe retreat would long ago have yielded up the lean bull-nosed trout to some enterprising and covetous depredator. Reining up his horse,

John Wharton looked down the village, and thought how utterly rural and distinctly agricultural the village looked; yet almost within ear-shot of the machinery, the hum of spindles of the huge cotton-mills.

Riding on he encountered a cart-load of hay, fragrant and sweet, drawn steadily along by a sleepy horse; while by the cart strode a man in his shirt-sleeves, hot and perspiring with his efforts in the hayfield. The hedges were thick and scrambling, protected by outlying masses of gorse or bramble; every now and then a spray of the dark purple flowers of the deadly nightshade might be seen intertwined with the prickly branches of the sloe-thorn. Then came the sweet odour of the honey-suckle (so dear to the hearts of small children), with its curious flowers, unique of their kind. By a turn in the road one of the Peak mountains came into view, bare and brown with its dry, sunburnt grass. The road now was deeply cut into the ground, and some feet of bank existed before the

hedgerow began. Ferns and mosses, ground-
ivy, and herb-robert grew freely. Amidst
this wealth of green carpet could be seen,
here and there, little tufts of spleenwort.
John Wharton could not help contrasting
the luxuriance of this undergrowth with the
comparative bareness of the hedgerows at
Brigstone. But he missed the holly fences,
which were so common at home; and also
the tall spikes of the purple fox-glove. The
road now became level, and Hawk seemed
to think that a trot would be agreeable, so
communicating his wishes to his rider—as
horses can—he set off at a round pace until
Black Edge came into sight on the right of
the road. The road now began to slope
upwards, with the Peak Forest on the left.
Soon the mountain aspect began to obtain,
and inquiry of a wayfarer told John Wharton
he was nearing his destination.

His mind now left the hedgerows as his
eye took in the widening scene. Hills
grew up as he mounted the slope. A wide
expanse opened out—the high ground of

Buxton with the Peak mountains in the distance. Sheep were seen plentifully scattered over the scanty herbage,—the short grass sheep love so well. Here and there was a shaggy pony; while a few Irish cattle with the white streak along the back-bone were in sight, grazing industriously without a disturbing suspicion of the butcher's knife. Soon the houses of Buxton came in sight, and John Wharton had to make several inquiries before he could arrive at the desired information, viz. the whereabouts of Peak Cottage.

'Who lives thear?' asked one man evidently anxious to aid the stranger.

'Mr. Carlyon. A fine-looking, white-haired old gentleman. Tall and stout.'

'Th' ould gentleman that distributes th' trac's about the Corn Laws.' John Wharton thought it highly probable that if there was one gentleman only who disseminated views opposed to the Corn Laws at Buxton, that individual would in all probability be Hugh Carlyon.

'Yes; that is the gentleman. How are the tracts received?'

'Oh, th' folk care little about them. They just tek them to please him, and his bonnie daughter. They are a gradely pair! His hoose is just round to the left; the neame's on th' gate-post.'

Thanking the man for his civility and his information, the traveller turned to the left; and soon came upon a handsome house, with a well-kept, if small, lawn, and mullioned windows, over which trailed a slight evergreen — a double kerria with yellow flowers, few and sparse, the season being late for it. There was an air of newness, of wealth, and of thrift, blended, about the premises.

As John Wharton drew up at the gate a handsome young lady came to the window, but quickly started back; not before the stranger had seen enough to corroborate his informant's opinion about Miss Carlyon's appearance. His thoughts, however, had not wandered more than a second or two before Mr. Carlyon was to be seen opening the front-door, and hastening to the gate to give his visitor an old-fashioned, hearty welcome.

'Glad to see you, landowner and re-former!' he exclaimed. After shaking hands cordially : 'Have you had a pleasant ride ? You have a powerful horse,' he said. His eye wandered over Hawk's proportions with the keen scrutiny of a man who loves horseflesh. 'About as useful a horse as I have seen for some time. I'll call the groom, and have him put up. There is plenty of room, and he won't be miserable at Buxton ; whatever you may be. There is going to be a Chartist meeting on Friday : that will be an attraction for you, at any rate.'

'Got up for the occasion, I suppose ?'

'Not exactly ; as they did not know you were coming. Have you anything beyond the waterproof ?' pointing to a roll strapped to the saddle in front.

'There is a little thing or two wrapped in it. One cannot take a large wardrobe with one on horseback.'

'Not very well. Now dismount. Your horse sniffs the groom in an inquiring manner. Is he quiet?'

'Perfectly ; but Hawk does not take up with people off-hand. He likes to make up his mind about them.'

'He and Tom will get on famously, I doubt not. Come in and let me look after you. We are old-fashioned, and dine in the middle of the day ; but there will be cold meat, or something. I remember some potted trout at breakfast. We'll find you enough.'

'My wants are not extensive. Don't let me give you any trouble.'

'My daughter knew of your coming. She is a pretty good housewife. Let me introduce you to her.'

The introduction was made, and it was announced that tea would soon be ready.

'Have a glass of wine till tea is ready. You must want something after your journey.'

'Not any, I thank you. I take very little wine.'

' How's that ? '

' Because I do not care about it.   A little claret is all I take, as a rule.'

' Well, we have some, fortunately.   May, see there is some claret got out.   You find us here in a very plain way.   We only have the house furnished for the summer, and it does not make too much work for the housekeeper in winter.   It's no use making work, you know.'

John Wharton looked around him.   He was in the dining-room,—the main living room.   The furniture was plain, substantial mahogany, covered with black horse-hair : a sofa, two arm-chairs, a few ordinary chairs.

' Perhaps you would like a wash.   Come along, and I will show you your bed-room.'

Mr. Carlyon led the way.   Again the furniture was plain.

' You will find us in the drawing-room.'

So saying, Mr. Carlyon left his guest, who looked at his waterproof with its scanty contents.

'Rather short of linen, I am afraid. Perhaps I can buy some. Nice pleasant girl, Miss Carlyon : keeps the house neat. I wonder if she is to be my " fate, " as Edie put it ? Well, I shall accept it without grumbling if such has to be the end of it. Wonder if she has any brothers or sisters ? '

Whether he thought wondering or inquiring the more practical solution of the problem may be settled by the fact that he was not long in finding his way into the drawing-room.

Here he found Mr. Carlyon and his daughter.

' You are not a large family, Mr. Carlyon,' he said, curious to know the facts.

' No : there are only my daughter and myself. We do not require a large establishment ; and I hate a lot of servants getting into each other's way,—running over each other professing to wait on me. We are very comfortable for the summer.'

While he was speaking, John Wharton ran his eye over the room. It also had no

superfluous furniture: what there was consisted of walnut covered with a pretty light
chintz. There were a few pieces of needle-
work here and there.

' You share in your papa's views about
politics, Miss Carlyon?'

' I? yes. How do you know?'

' I had to ask for Peak Cottage; and my
informant inquired if I meant the gentleman and his daughter who give away tracts
on the Corn Laws. I thought that must be
your papa, at any rate.'

' How curious! That was his description
of us. You see, papa, how we are known.'

' I see no objection to the description, do
you?'

' Certainly not. One likes to know how
other people—as one's neighbours, for
instance—regard one.'

While this dialogue was proceeding, John
Wharton looked at Miss Carlyon. She was
tall, slight, with good features and a clear
complexion. Her hair, like her eyes, was
dark brown, and drawn away from her face

and wreathed in plaits on the top of her
head. Her brow was lofty; her eyebrows
well marked, but forming only a thin line;
her nose was shapely, straight, with a delicate outline; her ears thin and shell-like;
her mouth small, with a slightly full under-
lip; teeth small but well-formed; the chin
light. It was a bright, engaging, and
attractive face, which looked happy; though
a slight frown came over it at times, telling
of a hasty temperament. The head was
small and distinctly oval, and the same
might be said of the face. The hands were
shapely, but rather large hands. They
looked competent hands; not afraid of
work evidently. The long fingers told of
artistic power; and Miss Carlyon could
handle a pencil as well as a needle,—and that
she certainly could wield. She looked as if
she could form opinions of her own, and, having formed them, hold and maintain them.

"Are you merely an Anti-Corn Law
repealer, or have you wider sympathies,
Miss Carlyon ?'

'What do you mean by "wider sympathies," Mr. Wharton? I do not quite
understand you.'

'Are you a reformer? Do you wish to
see the people properly represented in
Parliament?'

'Do you mean, am I a Chartist?'

'Yes; if you choose to put it that way.'

'Then I am very doubtful about my
position. You see I am a woman; and, as
such, timid. And the tales one hears and
reads about, of armed gatherings, and pikes,
and cats,—whatever these last are,—make
one a little afraid.'

'You fear violence! You may say so
without laying yourself open to the charge
of cowardice. It is the ill-luck of the
Chartist movement to have attracted to it
all the insubordinate elements of society.
But that does not affect the principle of
the movement.'

'I cannot follow you properly. I know
little about the principle. Papa says it is
an impracticable project. And some very

good people I know denounce it as rebellion
under disguise, and say the Chartists are
infidels.'

' Oh, that is what the Pharisees say.'

' Pharisees! I did not know there were
any Pharisees now.'

' They do not go by that name. But
the nature of the beast is the same,—whatever name it bears.'

It was quite clear that an element of
danger to the harmony of Peak Cottage
was being introduced in these plain-spoken
words. Ladies do not like their friends,
who are respectabilities, to be spoken of
as Pharisees ; and Miss Carlyon was inclined
to feel a little shocked, though no Miss
Nancy. Mr. Carlyon thought it well to
interrupt the conversation.

' Is tea ready, my dear ? Perhaps Mr.
Wharton will have no objection to have a
drive with us in the evening ? There are
some sights at Buxton which you must
see. What do you say ? '

' I shall be delighted.'

So tea was served with some savoury cold morsels, suited to the appetite of a man who has had a long ride on a hot July day. Miss Carlyon was, as a house-wife, all her father had said for her.

Soon the open carriage and a pair of horses were waiting at the gate ; and, taking their seats, the trio drove round by the Crescent, then to Poole's Hole Cavern, and after that to the Diamond Hill (the ' Buxton diamonds,' viz. quartz crystals), and the ' Lover's Leap.' The conversation kept clear of any dangerous topics, and all were pleased with each other.

CHAPTER IX.

MORAL FORCE CHARTISTS.

NEXT day an excursion was made to the 'Cat and Fiddle,' on the Macclesfield road. This famous hostelry is the highest inhabited house in England; being higher than the little ale-house at the top of Kirkstone Pass, betwixt Ambleside and Patterdale, in the lake country. It was proposed that they should all go in the carriage; but John Wharton pleaded that Hawk would rather be out of doors than remain in the stable all day. So he rode beside the carriage. It was another beautiful day, and the breeze tempered the heat. The horses were put up while the three had a stroll. The conversation was animated. After a while Miss Carlyon said :

'Mr. Wharton, if you will not talk of "Pharisees," and use such very plain Saxon, I should like to hear a little more of the principle of the Charter. I feel interested.'

'I am delighted to hear you say so. But I must, in turn, request you to refrain from calling God-fearing people "infidels;" that is a little strong, don't you think?'

'I was only repeating what I heard. It was very stupid of me. But we will avoid strong language in future!'

'Here is a little bank and a pleasant view. Let us sit; and I will expound this matter to you.'

They sat down, and John Wharton gave Miss Carlyon a sketch of the whole movement in accordance with what has been laid down in Chapter XI., Vol. I.; and therefore need not be repeated. With feminine ardour she protested she thought the movement a good one. Her father admitted the arguments, but explained:

'It is not the principle I object to; it

is the magnitude of the demand. They can never get it all; and they will not take a piece at a time. We attack the Corn Laws and nothing else : and we will get their repeal after a while. The points of the Charter will come piecemeal, I believe, in time. But I have no faith in it as it stands at present.'

'I quite admit what you say. But if the principle is right, I think we are justified in fighting for it; fighting peacefully, of course.'

'Ay; but there is the rub! You have got a fighting element in your ranks.'

'That is true, I am sorry to say. And none regret it more than the moral-force Chartists themselves.'

'Will you speak at the meeting, Mr. Wharton? I should like to hear you expound your views in public,' broke in Miss Carlyon.

'I am no public speaker by habit; but I am willing to try.'

It is curious how young love can show itself. Here is Miss Carlyon, who is no impulsive romantic young lady, asking John Wharton to speak in public; and he is equally ready to oblige her!

'If you do,' said Mr. Carlyon, 'I wish you would put the arguments so as to contrast the movement with what was said and done by the advocates of the Reform Bill in 1831.'

'On Mr. Macaulay's line; will that do?'

'Capitally; he is a staunch Whig. You could not do better.'

After their return Mr. Carlyon took John Wharton to the workshop of a leading Chartist, Frank Cheadle, a master carpenter; who was glad to see so unwonted a supporter of the Charter; and, without any prompting, asked him if he would say a few words at the meeting.

'We talk among ourselves you see, sir, till we pretty well know what each other has to say. We should be glad of a new speaker; he would give us some new arguments.'

'Mr. Carlyon thinks it would be well to take some of the arguments of the Whig advocates of the Reform Bill, and apply them to the present time. What do you say to that line?'

'I think it a very good one. It will do famously.'

'The meeting is to-morrow (Friday) at seven in the evening?'

'Yes; we are all working-folk; we never meet till the day's-work's done. We waste no time over politics; whatever our opponents may say of us.'

The gentlemen turned away, and Frank Cheadle gleefully announced to his fellow-Chartists that evening, that a stranger, a gentleman 'from over Sheffield way,' who was a landowner, was going to speak at their meeting.

'We mun ha' th' band wi' us, we're like,' said one of a musical turn, and this was carried unanimously without a dissentient voice. They would show the gentleman such honours as lay in their power.

The evening came, and the meeting was held on an open space near Cheadle's shop.

A solid block of wood was put ready for the speakers to mount in turn. The news that the strange gentleman staying with Mr. Carlyon would speak, had been bruited abroad; and attracted a number of persons who under ordinary circumstances would have held aloof from the Chartist movement, as from an unclean thing. The real Chartists consisted of an inner ring of earnest, sober, thoughtful men, mechanics and the like. Two or three musical instruments were to be seen. When Mr. and Miss Carlyon had joined the group with their guest, Frank Cheadle mounted the block, and spoke as follows:

'You all know my views, so I need not repeat them here. We must have meetings in order to keep the pot boiling; and the Chartist pot must boil like other pots, else them as doesn't like it, will swear it's not warm. (Here a laugh went round the crowd.) Well, whether we are at boiling point or not, we're warm anyhow! We believe that the country needs reform; and

if we can get other folks to believe with us
we'll win. We are constantly told that we
have had enough of reform. That's what
they say that are represented in Parliament.
We are not; and we want to be! When
we are represented, then perhaps we will
be satisfied to rest and be thankful too.
We working men helped the Whigs to
carry the Reform Bill; believing that when
there was wider representation, the middle
class would help us in turn to get representation. But, as ye all know, we have not
had faith kept with us. We want fairation;
that's all we want! That the excesses of
the "physical force" men, or maybe I
should call them "lads," i' the great towns
have brought discredit upon us all, must be
admitted : and right sorry we true reformers
all are that such is the case. But the
principle is sound, I say ; and there is a
gentleman going to address us who is not
ashamed to join the people in trying to get
their rights. Them as say that "the Chartists" are the "narrow cloth," and the

Government the " broad cloth " folks may be right i' the main ; but there's exceptions even to that rule. I won't detain you longer, and will ask the gentleman to come forward.'

There was a brief pause, and it seemed to the musical element appropriate and befitting the occasion to indulge in a little of their favourite exercise. So they struck up one of Bramwich's hymns, of which this is the last verse :

'All men are equal in His sight,
The bond, the free, the black, the white :
He made them all,—them freedom gave ;
God made the man—man made the slave !'

This was sung fervently ; and though the crowd was a rather humble one there was little of 'slavery' in their holding an open meeting undisturbed by 'their gory oppressors ;' as some of the Chartists were in the habit of terming the authorities.

After the music ceased John Wharton walked quietly up to the block, and took his stand upon it. He looked round from

his elevation, and nodding to Mr. Carlyon
(possibly Miss Carlyon was included), he
began in clear tones :

'Friends, I should like to draw your
attention to some points in connection with
the demand for further Reform, known as
" the Charter," and the Chartist movement.
Let us follow the arguments used by Mr.
Macaulay in the debates which preceded
the passing of the Reform Bill, which he
said was "this second Bill of Rights, this
greater Charter of the Liberties of England,"
and see how they apply to the present case.
If they were sound, as regards the middle
classes, then enfranchised, I cannot see why
they are not sound as regards the classes
still left without the franchise. The working classes have been allowed to sit at a
Barmecide feast : they helped, and very
materially, these middle classes to the
franchise ; and then were left unaided to
clamour for their enfranchisement in turn.
That the Reformed Parliament has achieved
many great and most desirable legislative

measures—has indeed manifested a great and wholesome activity—is, to my mind, an argument for further extension of the franchise; not for standing still. (Loud applause.)

'But to return to the arguments used by a staunch Whig, a Whig of Whigs, "the people's friends." He said the voice of great events was proclaiming to us reform, that we might preserve. It was because the French aristocracy resisted reform in 1783, that they were unable to resist revolution in 1789. It was because they clung too long to odious exemptions and distinctions, that they were at last unable to save their lands, their mansions, their heads. They would not endure Turgot, the King's minister; and they had to endure Robespierre and the guillotine. To extend the franchise was, in 1831, held to be robbery of those who already possessed it. Representation, it was stated, belonged to the land and its owners; rather than to the people. How did he dispose of this statement ? " You tell the people that it is as unjust to disfranchise a great lord's nomination-borough as to confiscate his estate. Take heed that you do not succeed in convincing weak and ignorant minds that there is no more injustice in confiscating his estate than in disfranchising his borough." He told them not to "bind together two totally different things. Foolish minds will do so, and their weakness and folly bear their appropriate fruit." Their boroughs have been disfranchised, and their argument has recoiled upon them. A considerable class in the nation would have no objection to confiscate their property ; but a larger, a wiser, and stronger class, forbid their doing so. These speeches have led the discontented classes to talk of confiscation. This has been the direct outcome of their own feeble arguments against reform. But it has not been enough that they have stirred up folly and wickedness by their speeches ; they 'have done worse. They have sent out by design agitators to mislead the people, to lure them on the course of wickedness and crime. Have not Chartist speakers inciting to violence been found to have really been Government emissaries and spies? And then the passions of the people are blamed for it all. It stirs one's blood within one's veins to know of such devices, — such infamous artifices !

'Then it is argued that if the franchise is exte nded, common, incapable, coarse men will be returned to Parliament. Let us see how Mr. Macaulay meets this assertion that none but mob-orators,—men that are willing to pay the basest court to the multitude, will have any chance of being returned. He asked them to look at Nottingham—with a franchise lower than that proposed by the advocates of the Reform Bill,—where they would see two distinguished men, not connected with the town at all, its representatives in the House of Commons. Look at Leicester, he said, where every man paying "scot and lot" has a vote. Who are the members for Leicester? A Tory baronet, and a manufacturer linked with other counties. Look at Northampton with a franchise lower even than " scot and lot "; were the members for Northampton slaves of the mob? Who have been the members for Westminster and Southwark? Have they been above or below the average members of Parliament? From Mr. Fox to Sir Samuel Romilly, who never even showed himself upon the hustings; have they been mob-orators? Where is the validity of that argument? Well may Lovett and Collins write from Warwick gaol: " The candidates who have been elected by the multitude by a show of hands have been better qualified for their respective offices, both intellectually and morally, than those who were subsequently elected by the privileged class of voters." I do not see how the arguments apply less now than they did then.

Then it was argued that it was not wise to yield before popular commotion. What did he point out? Why, that the whole history of England was the history of Government giving way before a people that is constantly advancing. Charles I. only tried to rule like Henry VIII., but the Englishmen of 1640 were not the Englishmen of 1540. He forgot the advance that had been made; and he lost his head as the consequence of his forgetfulness. The Government of Louis XVI. was a milder, better Government than that of Louis XIV.; but Louis XIV. was "the grand monarch," while Louis XVI. perished on the scaffold. Changes in society must be followed by changes in the Government. Yes, he said: "You may make the change tedious, you may make it violent, you may even make it bloody; but avert it you cannot." Despite the opposition of the Lords and borough-owners the Reform Bill was passed. (Applause.)

'Then as now it was pleaded: "Would you alter the representative system in such agitated times?" What was the Whigs'

answer ? " Reformers are compelled to legislate in times of excitement because bigots
will not legislate in times of tranquillity."
We are compelled to move fast because
they would not move at all. If any bad
consequences should follow from the haste
and excitement, let those be held answer-
able who, when there was no need of
haste, when there existed no excitement,
refused to listen to any project of reform ;
nay, who made it an argument against
reform that the public mind was not excited.   Half the logic of misgovernment
lies in this one sophistical dilemma :   If
the people are turbulent they are unfit for
liberty ; if they are quiet they do not want
liberty."   Now, if these arguments were
valid in 1831, in favour of reform ; I cannot see how they have lost their weight in
eight short years, and are not equally valid
now ?   (More and louder applause.)

   ' That the opponents of reform gave way
at last before the arguments used, and
beyond and behind these arguments the

popular will, is a matter of history. We are now told to rest and be thankful ; that there should be no national disquiet.

'"We ought to wait," says "Finality John." (Laughter.) Again, let us see what was the Whig argument then. Is delay no evil? Is prolonged excitement no evil? Is it no evil that the heart of a great people should be made sick by deferred hope? We allow that many of the changes that have been made are improvements. Have there been no improvements made by the reformed parliament? Improvements enough to warrant more reform, I hold. Whenever great interests are at stake there will be much excitement; and wherever there is much excitement there will be some extravagance. Is this less true now than it was eight years ago? Have we not foolish agitators now who tell the working-classes much that is to be deplored? And if the masses are ignorant and easily misled, whose fault is it? Is it all their own? They are what their situation has made them : ignorant from want of leisure ; irritable from the sense of distress. That they should be deluded by impudent assertions and gross sophisms ; that, suffering cruel privations, they should give ready credence to promises of relief ; that, never having investigated the nature and operations of Government, they should expect impossibilities from it, and should reproach it for not performing impossibilities : all this is perfectly natural. It was "perfectly natural" then : but do these very Whigs allow it to be "perfectly natural" now ?

' "Pain and sorrow can make us very querulous and very unreasonable," it was pleaded then. Have the people no pain, no sorrow now ? When want is stalking about ; when the Leicester weaver can only earn four-shillings-and-sixpence a week, and wheat is seventy shillings the quarter ! The landed interest protects itself by legislative measures which make bread dearer for the starving people ; and then expects that they should be free from a sense of wrong ? I am connected with the landed interest ; but that does not blind me to a sense of right and wrong. I am not surprised that when the land is thus protected by legislation, a certain portion of the ignorant starving masses should clamour for a return to the old Poor Law; that they should threaten to resort to violence ; that indeed in some quarters they should have been tempted to violence. It is much to be deplored that they should have been tempted to resort to violence ; violence does no good, but much harm. But if the Government would do something to relieve the starving man it would pacify him. If they would let him have bread at a price bearing some reasonable proportion to his wages, it would allay much of the general discontent. That at least the Government might do. The people are quite as important as the land. If the people could see the Government trying to help, in their trouble, then they in turn would become more reasonable. That they will still seek their rights is certain.

They will not abandon the Charter when
the Anti-Corn Law League has done away
with the tax on bread ; but the bread-tax
is a terrible burden on a starving people !

' It has been asserted that the people will
indemnify themselves by illegal excesses for
the want of legal privileges. There have
been riots, chiefly by crowds maddened by
hunger ; and there may be more in the
future. It is because our rulers have no
sympathy with the people ; no discernment
of the signs of the times ; no share in their
hunger ; that the masses are raging, and in
revolt even. The demagogue would have
no audience but for the just indignation
excited among the multitude by the inso-
lence of the enemies of reform : and the last
hope of the enemies of reform lies in the
uneasiness that is excited among all who
have anything to lose, by the ravings of the
demagogue. Yes ; and I ask, while my
cheek burns with shame,—Englishman as I
am,—how many of these demagogues are
Government agents ?

' Have the early reformers or Chartists either advocated or used violence at their meetings? Was there any rioting when the first Chartist meeting was held in London, in February 1837? We must seek redress by legal means. Reform is not revolution. Revolution does not belong to the order-loving people of England: they seek reform by constitutional measures. We seek what they sought in 1831, namely, a peaceful,—a lawful reform. The natural distribution of power, and the legal distribution of power, are not in proportion to each other. They should be! It is dangerous, they say, to give power to the people who are unfit to make a wise, or prudent use of it. Are the people of England less fit for self-government than the people of Switzerland, or the United States? Yet none of those terrible results which are so confidently prophesied for England in the event of further reform, and extension of the franchise, have yet happened to either

of these free countries. I do not believe Englishmen less fit to govern themselves than these two nations. I utterly
disbelieve it. I feel sure these fears are
groundless. (Cheers.) In conclusion, I say
that I do not see what has occurred to alter
arguments which were valid in 1831, and
render them of no weight now. It may
be my inability to recognize some essential
difference betwixt then and now; but I
see none. Our reasons are as sound as
those of the Whig reformers; and our proceedings ought to be the same, viz. an
appeal to reason, to justice. No pike-heads
and fire-raisings. "Peace, law, and order;"
that must be our motto! An Englishman
has a right,—a free Englishman, that is
neither felon nor pauper,—has a right to a
voice in the making of the laws that govern
him; as it was with our Saxon ancestors,
when they first came to our shores; and all
the powers under heaven cannot prevent his
having such voice sooner or later. Was
earth made for the few, or the many? Is

it reasonable that the few shall make the laws for the many? Whither have the deeds of the reformed parliament pointed? are questions to be asked. Not to rest: but to more reform, I say! But let us attain our ends by legal means; or not at all!' (Loud applause.)

The band then struck up, while the crowd sang:

> 'Then rouse, my boys, and fight the foe;
>   Your arms are truth and reason;
>   We'll let the Whigs and Tories know
>   That Union is not treason.
>   Ye Lords, oppose us if you can,
>   Your own doom you seek after;
>   With, or without you we will stand,
>   Until you give the Charter.'

After which 'groans for "Finality John"' were given; and the sounds were not unlike those of a ranters' meeting, when a conviction of sin was felt by a multitude who had suddenly awakened to a living belief in the fact that they had souls to be saved. Then 'three cheers for the speaker;' after which the meeting broke up. The opinions expressed by the speaker were eagerly discussed by various members of the Chartist body.

'Do ye say he comes from Sheffield way? I thought the "physical force" men were strang thear. He's no "physical force" man, I reckon. He wound Macaulay up to a tidy tune. The arguments of 1831 won't suit 1839. The Whig Government is about worn out with what it has achieved. It's time for new blood, I say. The Charter we must hev', and if the Whigs won't give us it; why, we will see what the Tories can do. It's like they'll win i' the next 'lection,' was the comment of a sturdy quarry-mason.

'That's the kind o' talk we want more on. None o' yer nonsense about "pikes an' feightin'," or even "the sacred month," and sich-like rubbish,' said a blacksmith.

John Wharton joined Mr. and Miss Carlyon, slightly excited by his unwonted exercise.

'You hit it off capitally. Just enough, and not too much,' said the old gentleman.

'I am afraid I have not been doing you justice, Mr. Wharton. You quite exceeded my expectations,' Miss Carlyon said.

'Then your expectations had not gone very high, I fear?'

'On the contrary. I formed rather lofty expectations; but I had no idea you were such an accomplished speaker. You quite impressed your audience, I could not help observing.'

Miss Carlyon may not have been a very competent, or even impartial, critic; but John Wharton felt just then what many another man has experienced, viz. that the approbation of a lady is sweeter and more acceptable to the palate, than the like approval from any number of male lips, when something has been done.

Stump oratory on such a dry subject as 'political reform' is a curious mode of courtship; yet little Cupid was fluttering over that block, and shot a barbed arrow right into Miss Carlyon's heart.

When she made her complimentary speech

the little joker took aim again. No one
heard the twang of his bow-string, no eye
caught sight of the arrow in its flight;
but it transfixed John Wharton : but the
feathered shaft could not be seen projecting
by the side of the heavy lapel of his coat on
the left side.   It was evidently deeply
buried.

Eros, God of love! what sport thou
makest with human hearts!

CHAPTER X.

OTHER CHARTISTS.

NEXT morning a change in the weather seemed threatening, and the Carlyons felt it no want of hospitality to speed the parting guest.

'Can you not manage to find your way here again before the season closes, now that you have found us out?' asked Mr. Carlyon, cheerily.

'And he might bring Miss Wharton with him, papa, I am sure,' continued Miss Carlyon.

'Right, my dear. Can you not promise to bring your sister too? Say about the first week in September. Come, promise me?'

There was no doubt about the genuineness of the invitation; and as he, personally, had no objection to keep up his familiarity with the Carlyons, John Wharton promised to see what could be done.

Hawk was eager to be off, so amidst friendly 'adieus' the stranger turned homewards. He moved on more rapidly than he had travelled on his outward journey, as clouds were gathering. Hawk was ready for a rest at Glossop, after which he set off with a sturdy determination to get home as speedily as possible. The rain began to descend as they reached the summit of the moors, and soon came down heavily. Fortunately they had the rain on their back, else it would have been very disagreeable.

'We must ride for it, Hawk. You can have a good rest to-morrow:' his horse seemed to understand perfectly what the rider said, and was not long in turning into the yard at Fowrass Grange. Luke Ellwood was on the watch for the pair, and when he heard the horse's footsteps went out gleefully to meet them.

'Ye've brought a change i' th' weather wi' ye, sir,' was the greeting. 'Th' rain will suit us well; but it'll do th' corn na good.' So saying he helped his master to dismount.

'All well, Luke?'

'Ay; ivverything,' was the equally curt reply; for it was no time for parleying.

After a hasty greeting with his sister, John Wharton divested himself of his besplashed riding attire; and settled down for a quiet evening as the rain fell in an unbroken downpour. Miss Wharton listened eagerly to all details about the Carlyons; and the speech.

'Why, Jack,' she said, 'whatever induced you to make that speech? Uncle will not like it.'

'To tell the truth, I was not thinking of him at the time. Perhaps he will not hear of it.'

'I hope he will not; for I am sure he would be annoyed.'

'Dear uncle, I am afraid my views are unpalatable to him; but I cannot help that.'

'We need not vex him more than we can help. What did the Carlyons say to your speech, Jack?'

'They were pleased with it.'

'Miss Carlyon. Did she say anything?'

'Yes; she complimented me on it.'

'I told you how it would be.'

'Nonsense! women always detect court-ship, if two unmarried people get on well together. They want me to visit them again, and to take you with me. Do you think you could ride there in a day? The distance would not be too much for Daisy.'

'I shall have to consider some other matters than Daisy. Inviting me looks significant. Miss Carlyon is smitten, Jack!'

'Go away with you. You are so fond of your brother you think every other woman ought to be equally so. That's nonsense!'

'So she should be too ; if she has any taste,' said Miss Wharton, turning away to the door in pursuance of some domestic object; adding to herself when out : 'A man never sees a thing till it hits him on the bridge of his nose. The gentleman's sister is to be brought on the scene, that the ladies may take the measure of each other. Yes ; it looks like a match ! I hope I shall like Miss Carlyon. I should like to see the dear old boy happily married. Then I could leave him with a good conscience.'

The rain came down steadily till a flood of unusual height was the result : and the consequence of the weather was damage to the corn crops, and a rise in the price of corn.

The Chartists of Sheffield had been active all this time, holding meetings of their own constantly ; while disturbing the peaceful meetings of the Corn Law agitators, and indeed making themselves felt everywhere. They had become aggressive even ; and at their meetings, which were held nightly, the names of the tradesmen of the town who subscribed to their funds were read over, as well as the names of those who declined to do so. The latest idea of the advanced Chartists was to fix a 'sacred month' to be devoted to meetings and demonstrations. August was the month fixed upon as being on the whole the most convenient. Then the members of Parliament could give an account of their actions during the past session; and be returned again, or rejected, according to their stewardship. The elections were to be held then; and indeed it was to be the political month par-excellence. On August 6th they held a meeting in Paradise Square, at which the following resolution was carried :

'That this meeting, while we believe that nothing less than an universal stand can get the Charter, we believe that this town and district are not yet sufficiently organized for the adoption of the " sacred month ;" but nevertheless we wait the decision of

the General Convention, and pledge ourselves to adopt and carry out all measures
UNCONDITIONALLY recommended by them
for securing the people's Charter.'

There was more than mere defiance of the
authorities in their meetings, and after the
meetings and processions almost unbroken,
and occupying the whole of the 12th, the
magistrates issued a proclamation forbidding
such meetings. Two men who had made
themselves very conspicuous by their conduct were apprehended, and brought before
the magistrates. The consequence was
that there was a serious riot on the 13th,
and the military were called to the aid of
the police ; and many persons were injured
though no one was killed, and some scores
of rioters were apprehended. The town
was almost in a state of siege. The working classes were by no means all bitten
by Chartism, and some thousands offered
themselves as special constables, and their
services were accepted. The chief portion
of the troops were called away to Maccles-

field, where matters were even worse, so the yeomanry were called out. Between the yeomanry and the agitators no love was lost. Force was being met by force.

On the Sunday following these events, the Chartists took a new departure, and attended the parish church, having requested the Vicar to preach from a particular text. He announced that next Sunday he should do so. When the time came he did as requested. The text chosen was the fifth chapter of St. James, up to the eleventh verse. For the convenience of readers who may not be familiar with St. James, or who may not have the reference at hand, it may be well to give it in its entirety.

'1 Go to now, ye rich men, weep and howl for your miseries that shall come upon you.

'2 Your riches are corrupted, and your garments are motheaten.

'3 Your gold and silver is cankered; and the rust of them shall be a witness against you, and shall eat your flesh as it were fire. Ye have heaped treasure together for the last days.

' 4 Behold, the hire of the labourers who have reaped down your fields, which is of you kept back by fraud, crieth : and the cries of them which have reaped are entered into the ears of the Lord of sabaoth.

' 5 Ye have lived in pleasure on the earth, and been wanton ; ye have nourished your hearts, as in a day of slaughter.

' 6 Ye have condemned and killed the just ; and he doth not resist you.

' 7 Be patient therefore, brethren, unto the coming of the Lord. Behold, the husbandman waiteth for the precious fruit of the earth, and hath long patience for it, until he receive the early and latter rain.

' 8 Be ye also patient ; stablish your hearts : for the coming of the Lord draweth nigh.

' 9 Grudge not one against another, brethren, lest ye be condemned : behold, the judge standeth before the door.

' 10 Take, my brethren, the prophets, who have spoken in the name of the Lord, for an example of suffering affliction, and of patience.

' 11 Behold, we count them happy which endure. Ye have heard of the patience of Job, and have seen the end of the Lord ; that the Lord is very pitiful, and of tender mercy.'

How the sermon progressed ; or what might be the objects of the Vicar in preaching from such a text may have been ; certain it is that with the town seething in unquiet and views running high in conflict, it could only add to the commotion. On the third Sunday there was such a disturbance that the Vicar and Churchwardens applied to the magistrates ' to claim the protection of the law against a recurrence of the painful scene which happened in the parish church on Sunday :' the outcome of the presence of the Chartists. The magistrates complied with the request, and on the next Sunday armed policemen were placed at the gates of the churchyard, and in the church itself, in order to prevent any rioting or disturbance; and were successful in keeping the peace. This may to some extent have been due to the fact that on the day after the application to the magistrates, the Chartists had held another 'silent' meeting in Paradise Square; had been dispersed by the police and the military; had assembled again at Doctor's Field; and being again dispersed, but not without much stone-throwing, in which numbers were severely injured, though none were killed. Over thirty prisoners were taken. A few of these were sent to York, but admitted to bail; while others had to enter into recognizances, and find sureties to keep the peace.

But even then the defiance of the authorities on the part of the 'physical force' Chartists was pronounced. An Irishman who had attended a seditious meeting had declared among other threats that 'if any magistrate dared issue a warrant against himself or his brothers, he would assassinate him by day or night;' and also with asking the meeting—'Is there a man amongst you who cannot make a blade that will draw blood?' He was committed for trial at York Castle. These remarks testify what a wild spirit of lawlessness had taken hold of a section of the Chartists.

The natural consequence of such a spirit was of course equally energetic action by those opposed to them. A large number of the more prominent advocates of violence were bound over to keep the peace, and so rendered quiet. The authorities also were firm in their determination to put down the meetings. A great meeting was to be held at Sky Edge; but on the Chartists becoming aware of the fact that ball-cartridge had been served out to the troops who would have to disperse them, it was thought prudent not to hold it. Held in check by the firm attitude of the authorities, the Chartists made themselves less conspicuous; but many feared they were all the more plotting mischief in secret.

The early part of the year had been unusually dry; but after midsummer a change took place in the weather, and August was wet; while the rainfall of September was very heavy, amounting to almost thirteen inches; in October the rain continued, and towards the latter portion of the month heavy rains fell for several days without intermission. The effects of such weather upon the harvest were disastrous. It was deficient both in quantity and quality; and though the bad quality kept the prices from rising very high, the duty, which on November 1st was eighteen shillings and eightpence per quarter, prevented the entrance of foreign corn of better quality.

At Brigstone the rain kept the harvesting operations back; and in the middle of October the harvest was progressing but slowly. The consequence was the prospects for the coming winter were exceedingly gloomy: and all were full of apprehension as to what would happen.

The Anti-Corn Law agitators were distinctly peaceful : an attitude which irritated the physical force Chartists into fierce opposition to them. The food-outlook roused both parties. The league against the Corn Laws redoubled its efforts The violent element of the Chartists spread terror over the land by their threats, and their general attitude.

The country was in consequence nearly beside itself with terror. Villages of a purely agricultural character like Brigstone, under the immediate eye of a magistrate of character and decision, were comparatively undisturbed : but even there the contagion of the alarm caused much internal uneasiness. At Wybrow there had been meetings in which much sedition had been talked, and many wild threats uttered. In Barnsley there had been scenes like those described as occurring at Sheffield ; where the Chartist, or insubordinate element had perpetrated several outrages.

In calling this lawlessness by the name of

Chartism, it must be clearly kept in mind that under the cloak of Chartist meetings and processions, many of the criminal class contrived to pursue their nefarious practices. Many of the more violent agitators and preachers of sedition were, it is sad and also shameful to have to confess, the paid agents of the ruling powers.

A writer belonging to the Protectionist party has described the Chartists as brawling for the rights of man ; while the Anti-Corn Law League preached a cheap-bread crusade. And under the cover of those who were in earnest, the rabble element of society carried on war against the property-holder of all kinds. While admitting this, there was more of violence than of plunder in the riotous doings of that unhappy time.

In Birmingham, even so early as in July, there had been grave riots ; in which not only had much glass been broken, but warehouses had been pillaged and their contents piled up in the streets, and set on fire, to make bonfires ; while in other instances houses had been fired.

One class had been the special object of the hatred of these riotous crowds, and these were the corn-merchants. These were especially obnoxious to all the agitators ; whether mere Anti-Corn Law people, or full-fledged physical-force Chartists. The character of the harvest had set these merchants to work speculating ; and no one was more energetic than Mr. Mortlake, one of the promoters of the Wybrow Bank. Threats had been uttered against him ; and it became pretty certain that an attempt would be made to mark the feeling against him, sooner or later. He himself professed to hold the Chartists and their threats in the utmost contempt. He refused to re-move his wife and children from his Wybrow residence, or even to take measures for their protection.

' Why should I make any special prepara-tions ? I am quite confident in the power of the authorities to protect me. Let them attack my house if they think fit to do so. As long as Canon Wordsworth is on the bench I am confident the majesty of the law will be maintained.' The consequence of this being that the intending rioters were infuriated by the taunting remark, and more determined than ever to make Mr. Mortlake feel their displeasure ; while Canon Wordsworth became an object of their detestation from being thus held as a rod in terror over their heads. They hated the Canon as an uncompromising upholder of law and rule. Muttered threats were thrown out, that he was not safe from their vengeance if they chose to march out to his house.

The backward state of the harvest, and the inferior quality of the corn from the bad weather, had caused wheat to run up in price, so that on October 1st it stood at seventy-five shillings and sixpence per quarter. An arrangement was made by some of the fiercer spirits in Sheffield and Barnsley, that they should go over one

night and head the Wybrow Chartists in
an attack on Mr. Mortlake's house. The
Wybrow police were by themselves utterly
unequal to any fight or resistance against
a mob; which mob was pretty certain to be
armed with bludgeons, if not with more
dangerous weapons. The secret was well
kept; and one night, as darkness fell, a
crowd seemed insensibly to gather round
a rallying-point. Sundry men were found
to wear crape masks, and it was clear some
serious mischief was afoot. Others were
seen with considerable-sized bundles, which
really consisted of oakum, which would
burn fiercely. At a given signal the mob
moved off towards Mr. Mortlake's house,
where the lighted windows made a ready
mark. The first intimation to the inhabit-
ants of danger to them brewing was a volley
of stones, smashing the windows of the
front of the house; followed instantaneously
by loud defiant cheers from the crowd. The
utmost dismay and alarm seized upon the
inmates. Mr. Mortlake was not at home,

if he had been, he could have done nothing. Mrs. Mortlake and the domestics, amidst frantic cries of ' Rioters ! ' ' The Chartists are on us ! ' ' Murder ! ' ' Police ! ' seized the children and fled from the back of the house shouting and screaming ; while the poor frightened children cried lustily in their alarm. Another volley of stones followed, and then the front door was forced open. The men in crape masks brought forward their bundles of tarred tow ; and placing them in the hall lighted the mass, flinging upon it chairs and things which would burn readily. The draught fanned the flames and carried them up-stairs ; and in a very short time the house was ablaze from ground-floor to attic. It was a villa residence standing in its own grounds ; and therefore its burning entailed an imaginary rather than a real danger of spreading to the adjacent houses. But to the inmates of these houses the danger seemed real enough ; and after snatching up such valuables as were portable, they fled from the scene.

The police were soon attracted to the spot, and could see the masked leaders leaping about exulting in their fiendish act, shouting and conducting themselves more like so many Red Indians than Englishmen. The light of the blazing house made every object clear and distinct; but at such distance as was deemed prudent the policemen could not distinguish any of the leaders of the outrage. The mob behind howled, and shouted encouragement to those actually engaged in firing the house; and kept together so as to prevent the police from getting nearer the actual offenders. The town was in an uproar, and the people nearly frantic. The authorities were power-less to act with such force as they had at command; and messengers were despatched to Sheffield and Barnsley for aid. Some of the more courageous of the special con-stables came forward, and it was determined to attempt an attack on the ring-leaders. But the organizers of the outrage knew their work too, and the attempts were baffled.

No efforts to reach the men who were wanted could pierce the negative resistance of the crowd; and as the roof fell in, and there was a momentary loss of light after the sparks had burnt out, the masked men disappeared. Sympathizers in the crowd kept them aware of the whereabouts of the police and the special constables; and soon it was understood they had escaped. Of course in the darkness each man could readily cast away his mask, and then there existed nothing to identify him with the act of arson. Some of the crowd had no great objection to be taken, knowing they had borne no active part in the deed, and so could not be severely punished; thus a number of prisoners were made. Rain soon came down heavily, and did away with any possible risk of the fire spreading. It also dispersed the crowd: and soon a heap of blackened ruins, with a red flame here and there, spluttering with the falling rain, and a deserted space around it, was all that met the eye. When the forces came up from Barnsley and Sheffield, all was over. Under the cover of the darkness and the rain, all traces of the perpetrators of the outrage were lost; and in the well-washed roads next morning there remained no foot-print to guide the police towards the where-abouts of the men they wanted. The Chartists had wreaked their vengeance upon Mr. Mortlake.

Next day a feeling of exasperation existed throughout Wybrow. The public were seized with that ferocity which is produced by fear, as well as desire for revenge. The deed was evidently carefully planned, and deliberately carried out; and as such de-serving of severe reprobation. When the magistrates assembled next morning they were fully impressed with the imperative necessity for such action as would be deterrent against the repetition of such outrage. Canon Wordsworth and Squire Wharton were strongly of this opinion; while Squire Oldfield naturally resented the

injury done to his fellow-shareholder in
the bank.

The half-dozen prisoners seemed inclined
to regard their night's residence within the
lock-up as part of the freak; and fully
expected that when no evidence tending to
connect them with the act of arson was
forthcoming, they would be discharged.
But they very soon found out the magistrates were in no humour to look at the
matter in that light. The Canon as chairman commenced by expressing his regret
that such an outrage had been perpetrated
at Wybrow; and that it was a most serious
offence, which must be dealt with in such a
manner as would show the seditious persons
of the neighbourhood that such acts could
not be regarded as trivial, but were grave
breaches of the peace. Squire Wharton
looked unusually stern,—an ominous indication for the culprits.

The evidence was then taken; first, that
of Mr. Mortlake, who deposed that many
threats had been made of what would be

done to him, and how he disregarded them ; trusting in the power of the law to protect him and his property : which last evidently told upon the chairman and Squire Wharton. Then the superintendent of the police described the stealthy manner in which the mob assembled ; and their superior numbers, before any suspicion was excited as to what was contemplated. How the actual offenders wore crape masks ; and how the crowd interposed so as to prevent them reaching the chief actors ; and also how they kept these actors aware of the whereabouts of the police and special constables. It was abundantly clear that the crowd thoroughly sympathized with the actual fire-raisers ; and did all that lay in their power to impede the police. The prisoners admitted being present in the crowd ; but pleaded they were only onlookers, and had taken no part in the outrage. They fully expected that under these circumstances they would be remanded for a week, for further evidence ; which would not be forthcoming, and then be discharged : they posing as heroes during the time of the remand. They were quickly undeceived, however. When the magistrates returned from considering their decision, the chairman, looking very serious, addressed the culprits as follows :

'We have given due and full consideration to the matter before coming to any conclusion. The offence is much more serious than the prisoners seem to realize. It is an offence of very great magnitude ; and must be dealt with accordingly. In these troublous times when there is a spirit of lawlessness abroad, we feel that we cannot deal with such an outrage as arson at the sessions. The prisoners must be tried before her Majesty's Judges, when the subject will be thoroughly sifted. The prisoners will then be tried by Judges who are perfectly impartial, and free from any local feeling. Under a recent Act of Parliament, the prisoners will have the advantage of being able to engage counsel to defend them; and who will be able to defend them,—who will be equal to making the most of any evidence which they may be able to bring forward in their defence. We do this in order to show the prisoners that we have no wish to press hardly upon them.'

The whole of them were then committed to York Castle, to be tried at the next gaol delivery,—the Winter Assizes.

The decision overwhelmed the prisoners and their friends. Two months must elapse before the Assizes came off, thus making sure of a term of imprisonment for them. Bail was promptly refused. There would be the loss of time,—a heavy fine; and, what was much more, there would be the cost of the defence, solicitors, counsel's fees, and the expense attendant upon getting together, and keeping for the requisite time at York, the necessary witnesses.

The Canon had professed the utmost desire to do justice to the prisoners, and yet the course taken entailed a very heavy punishment—even if they should be discharged at the Assizes. The magistrates had set an example of retaliation; and the Chartists and their sympathizers were enraged at the decision, and vowed vengeance in turn.

CHAPTER XI.

EVENTS MOVE ON.

THE weather was not very propitious for the proposed visit of John Wharton and his sister to the Carlyons; but it was determined to carry it out if it were possible. Pressing letters had been received from Mr. Carlyon, urging them to take advantage of any break in the rain to pay the visit.

Luke Ellwood took especial pains over Daisy, that she might look well, and bear the journey without exhaustion. It appeared to Luke that Buxton lay so far away that it seemed quite a long excursion; too far for Daisy in one day, even with Miss Wharton's weight upon her back.

' Puir little nag,' he would say ; ' it's a lang

journey for thee. I hope tho'll not be vary tired:' and when Daisy snuffed about for a crust in Luke's pocket, he said: 'I wonder if there'l be ennybody that will give thee a crust where thou's ganging till. I's feared not.' A fear on the kindly Luke's part which was quite groundless.

Warned by his previous experience, John Wharton had a small box of necessary articles of attire sent forward to Peak Cottage by the carrier, in readiness for their visit. If they did get caught in the wet on their journey it would not so much matter then.

The desired break came; and the two set off early one morning, and rode very quietly away to the summit of the moors, quickened their pace over them, and then made the descent quietly down to Glossop. John pointed out to his sister the various objects which he had noted on his previous ride. Miss Wharton enjoyed her ride very much; and the exertion brought a pleasing pink flush to her pale cheek. As before, a rest was made at Glossop; but, encumbered with her heavy riding-habit, Miss Wharton took a very cursory glance around the neighbourhood of the hostelry. As they reached the slopes of the Derbyshire hills she was struck with the profuse vegetation, and the wealth of the ground plants.

' Look, John, there is a perfect vegetable carpet. See how freely the harts'-tongues flourish! I have never seen anything like it: even at Stanmore — at least that I remember.'

Then when they came to the old Grange, and her brother pointed out how well it and the park-walls were designed for defensive military purposes, she was much impressed.

' I should think the people residing here are in no fear of the Chartists ?'

' I should think they have no reason to be afraid. The Chartists in rural districts are not of the violent order: they wish to do all peacefully, and stick by the laws.'

' I am sure I wish all of them would do the same !'

When they passed the gate and came to the village green, the overflow channels, almost dry on his previous visit, were seen to be running full with water.

'I wonder how my friend the bull-nosed trout is by this time. Fat and plump, I doubt not, if some angler has not caught him. The weather has been in his favour, anyhow,' John Wharton explained, as they rode over the bridge. It continued fine till they reached Buxton, but there were evidences of rain being about to fall.

Their greeting was most cordial; and both Mr. and Miss Carlyon were most solicitous in their care of Miss Wharton. Everything was ready for them; and, having removed all traces of their travel, they sat down to an appetising meal.

'I hope you have not forgotten your appetite, Miss Wharton. I am old-fashioned; and in my day it was always thought a good sign when a long ride sharpened the appetite instead of taking it away,' said Mr. Carlyon.

Miss Wharton thanked him warmly, and said she would let her actions speak for themselves.

Miss Carlyon and her guest soon got on good terms; and after tea sat at the window deeply immersed in a very serious feminine conversation,—in which matters domestic and articles of attire were alternately the topics. It was quite obvious that no difficulties would arise from differences so far as the ladies were concerned.

It was soon clear to Miss Wharton that the Carlyons were gentlefolks, though they preferred to live in their quiet way.

'You got a speech out of my brother when here before. I was so surprised when he told me. He has never shown any inclination to speak in public; I did not think it was in his line.'

'He spoke very fluently and easily, I assure you; and was listened to with the greatest attention. We have had many inquiries about him since then. He made quite an impression. Papa says he handled the matter very ably. I cannot presume to judge of that; but what he said seemed to me very convincing.'

Miss Wharton was delighted to hear her brother so spoken of; no more acceptable flattery could possibly have been offered to her. Whether the object of the praise was altogether unconscious of what was said of him or not, may not be affirmed; although to all appearance he was immersed in talking politics to Mr. Carlyon.

Two or three days passed very pleasantly, the weather permitting of excursions being made to several places of interest. Miss Carlyon rode well, and having succeeded in getting a pair of horses and the requisite riding gear, the Carlyons rode out with their guests. Naturally Mr. Carlyon waited upon Miss Wharton, leaving John Wharton to attend to Miss Carlyon. Mr. Carlyon admired Daisy very much, and said Mr. Wharton showed excellent judgment in horseflesh.

'It is a good point about a man to be a

good judge of a horse. It shows he can think for himself. Horsey men are a bad lot in my experience; too much horse is dangerous. But I like a man who knows a horse when he sees it,' was the old gentleman's comment.

Before the visit was over, Mr. Wharton had asked Mr. Carlyon's permission to pay his attentions to Miss Carlyon; with an old-fashioned sense of propriety. The consent was somewhat reluctantly given.

' It is not from any objection to you, Mr. Wharton, let that be clearly understood ; for, from what I have seen and heard of you, no man would wish a more eligible suitor for his daughter's hand,' explained the old gentleman; ' but from a selfish consideration. She is all I have. I lost Mrs. Carlyon ten years ago : it was a great trial to me. She left me with May and a son, as fine a young fellow as you would wish to see. He would join the army ; though I myself am rather a man of peace. His mother pleaded for him after she fell

ill, and I could not refuse her. He came
in his uniform to take a last farewell of her,
as she wanted to see him in it. And a
gallant young fellow he looked too in his
scarlet coat and gold lace. But unfortunately he was sent to Ireland, and got a
violent cold when on duty chasing Dan
O'Connell's followers, which ended in in-
flammation of the lungs. I went at once
on hearing the news; but I was too late:
he was dead when I got there.' Here the
old gentleman was silent from emotion for
a moment or two. 'Since then May has
been everything to me: and a better
daughter no father was ever blessed with.
But I must not be selfish; I must be
thankful if I find a son-in-law who will not
be a stranger to me, and with whom I have
much in common. I give you my permission to do so; but I will say nothing to
her. If you gain May's consent, you have
mine.'

This was readily agreed upon; and John
Wharton knew that he had an ally, if a

silent one, in Mr. Carlyon. He had great hopes of success with the lady.

The barometer rose one day, and it was agreed next morning to take their departure. The day before had been continuously wet, so they hoped for a fine day. It would be very wet under foot; but that mattered little as they were going home. The farewell was very earnest; and Miss Wharton thought she noticed Miss Carlyon's hand remained rather long in her brother's.

As they rode down the slope from Buxton, Miss Wharton said :

' Jack, it is getting serious.'

' What do you mean, Edie ?'

'The attachment between you and Miss Carlyon is evidently mutual; and I don't think Mr. Carlyon opposed to the match.'

' Would you have any objection ?'

' I ? Certainly none. She is a right down good girl, with a cultivated mind. She would make you an excellent wife. I have never yet met a girl so likely to make you a good wife.'

' I am very glad to hear you say so, Edie.
I have spoken to Mr. Carlyon, and he has
no objection to me.'

'Then it is as good as settled. I should
like to go a little faster, please.'

Having reached the flat, they rode steadily
on; John Wharton trotting, while Daisy
cantered by Hawk's side.

When they arrived at Glossop they were
well bespattered. The rain had come down
again; but it was clearly a shower only,
as they had watched the big black cloud
gathering nearer and nearer. It blew over;
and they set out, feeling pretty safe from
rain for the rest of the journey. When
Luke came out to take Daisy, he said:

' Whya puir little nag thou's o' mud!
And ye are jarbled, Miss!'

This last word rather puzzled Miss Wharton; but she judged it was one of Luke's
northern words for splashed.

After she had dismounted, he continued:

'Hev they treated thee weel, Daisy?
Thou shall be cleaned, and hev some clean

stra' and a gude warm mash to-neet at bed-time, that thou s'all.'

The groom looked rather carefully at Hawk ; and thought that a good hard job was before him, to make up for a day or two of idleness, before the horse and his riding-gear would be presentable.

When it became time to lock up the stables, the groom gave Hawk his usual feed ; while Luke brought the promised warm mash for Daisy.

' Thear now,' he said to her, ' that'll keep thee warm after thy lang journey. Thou'rt a good nag ! I wadn't see thee badly, or ail owt, for enything. Dost ti' like it ? Now then, here's a caake to finish wi' ;' with this he produced a sweet cake.

Luke and Annas were thrifty folks ; but they had been much exercised about Daisy, and feared she would not be well looked after : and Annas had been baking bread, and made a little cake with a dash of sugar in it, which she determined Luke should give her at bed-time. Luke was delighted at the considerate act. In answer to her inquiry how Daisy had received her offering, Luke said :

' Th' little nag can do ought but speak. She luiked at me sea knowingly efter she hed eaten'd caake, as much as to say, " I'm back hame, and I'm glad on't ! " '

Next day the two Whartons went over to Gaythorne Hall to see the Squire, and tell him how they had enjoyed their visit. He was glad to see them, and to know they were well. He showed a good deal of curiosity about Miss Carlyon.

' Is she a nice girl, Edie ? ' he asked.

' Uncommonly nice and sensible, uncle. And well-informed. I like her.'

' Well-informed, is she ? I suppose she shares her father's tastes, and reads a good deal ? I hear he is a strong Anti-Corn Law leaguer. I suppose she is so, too ? '

' I think she is, uncle. But they do not obtrude their views on their guests.'

' Well, that is a good thing. How does Jack get on with Miss Carlyon ? ' the old gentleman asked quietly, with a shrewd look upon his face.

'Very well. They are good friends.'

'Then I see what it will end in.'

Here John Wharton felt himself colouring very unpleasantly; and as it was clear his uncle noticed him reddening, the blush grew more pronounced.

'You need not say anything, Jack I can see. Well, I suppose it is the Marston blood,—but both to take up with reformers! It's hard on an old uncle that has no children of his own, and loves you both as well as if you were his own.'

It was useless to say anything. But the old Squire seemed troubled.

After a pause the conversation turned on what was going on in the neighbourhood.

'I fear we are going to have worse times than ever, Jack. These physical-force scoundrels are acting very unpleasantly at Sheffield; and things must be worse else-where: the troops were called to Maccles-field. Did you hear anything of what was doing there when at Buxton? It's not far from Macclesfield.'

'Not more than you would see in "The Times." There is a high ridge of mountains betwixt Buxton and Macclesfield. The silk-trade is in a very bad way, I believe. We must look out for disturbances this winter, I fear.'

'I have been thinking Edie would be as well out of the way for a month or two.'

'I am not afraid, uncle, I can assure you.'

'But I am for you. I am going to write to Cousin Barbara to take you till Easter. It will make a nice change for you.'

'But will it be convenient for her, uncle? She is getting old; and it may put her about?'

'If she is getting old it will be well to have you to wait on her. I shall write to-morrow. What do you say, Jack?'

'I do not think there is any danger of Fowrass Grange being attacked.'

'Perhaps not. But it seems you are not

so sure about Gaythorne Hall. They may try to burn the old man out; but I don't think an old soldier likely to be afraid of a lot of rebels. I have not forgotten the smell of gunpowder. We have a few fire-arms on the premises; and Bulman looks to them, and the ammunition too. We'll give them a warm welcome when they come.'

'I sincerely trust there may be no occa-sion to resort to Bulman's preparations. But of course lawlessness must be put down with a strong hand,' said John Wharton; glad to keep the conversation away from Buxton and Miss Carlyon.

The Squire communicated with the Lady Barbara Saville, who was delighted at the prospect of seeing her handsome young kinswoman again. She would be very glad to take her till Easter; or longer, if she could stay. The preparations for her visit were being pushed forward when the burning of Mr. Mortlake's house, and the threats uttered against Canon Wordsworth, caused them to be hastened vigorously.

The Chartists were exceedingly angry with the way the Wybrow rioters had been disposed of. The Bill allowing counsel to prisoners had only been passed a year or two before. Previous to that Act the prisoners would have had to defend themselves; and that, in this case with willing witnesses at hand, they could easily have done. But to have to take these witnesses to York, to keep them there, and pay counsel; the more the facts dawned upon them, the more they felt they had been out-manœuvred by the bench: and the more savage they became. Meetings of Chartists were quite common despite the orders of the magistrates against them; and one day a large force came out from Barnsley and joined the Wybrow Chartists: and a movement was made towards the Canon's residence, a little distance from Wybrow. 'Let's warm th' owd priest.' 'We'll fire 'un.' 'Th' owd hahse 'll burn like shavin's.' 'We'll teach 'im what a magistrate s'ud be.' 'We'll put 'im to th' cost of another hahse.' Such

were the cries from the crowd as they
surged along on their fiendish errand.
Friendly messengers hastened to the Canon's
to tell him what was on foot. The old
man's blood was soon up; and sending off
emissaries to bring the yeomanry from
Sheffield, he rode down to meet the rioters,
and read the Riot Act. This firm attitude
cowed many; while others began to see that
the consequences might be very disagreeable.

'You foolish fellows, turn back, I say!
You cannot master the rest of England, you
Chartists. The best men among you utterly
detest such proceedings. Go back, I say.'
He spoke in loud, clear tones. 'Go back, I
say; and not a man among you shall be
prosecuted.'

The promise affected the less courageous
and the more sensible,—or rather least reckless of the crowd; and a backward movement was commenced. The more desperate
of the leaders found themselves being deserted; and the Canon, scanning them carefully, thus addressed the knot of desperadoes :

‘ We will shoot you down if you attack my house. There are fire-arms in readiness, and the attempt will cost some of you your lives. Some of the rest will be wounded. and taken prisoners,—to be tried, and transported. I can swear to several of you. Now just turn back with the rest. It will be better for you.’ Sullenly and sulkily the remainder turned, and followed the main body. The Canon’s firm demeanour saved his house; and, what was more, saved bloodshed, and long terms of imprisonment for many of the foolish men.

But the moral effect of such a demonstration was tremendous. The alarm of all classes was intensified. A meditated attack might not be so successfully averted another time. The whole country-side was beside itself with terror. It was possible that an attempt might be made on Gaythorne Hall; for it was generally held by the Chartists that Squire Wharton had had a great deal to do with the decision of the bench.

'Th' Canon would nivver hev' dared to
due as he did, if Squire Wharton hadn't
backed him.'

That was the view taken by most of
those familiar with the circumstances.
And the feeling of irritation against the
Squire ran strong through the Chartist
ranks.

'Th' Squire hesn t forgitten th' murder
of Tom Earnshaw last winter. He bears
malice, th' Squire. He could find out
nought efter his reward, and he wanted
to pay off an ould score. That's what
meade him due as he did.'

There was no inherent improbability in
the supposition; and though the Squire
scoffed at the threats uttered, and Bulman
rather looked forward to a siege, so that
all his preparations might not be labour in
vain, it was thought very desirable to
get Miss Wharton away to the South;
where Chartism was, at that time at least,
less lawless. A rick or two might be
burned here and there, but nothing more.

There was none of that violence on a large scale which attached to the youthful mobs of the manufacturing towns.

At last the morning came for Miss Wharton's departure. She was to take the coach at Sheffield for Birmingham; stay all night at the latter town; and then proceed by the London and Birmingham Railway,—now opened through its entire length. Her brother would accompany her to Birmingham, and see her off in the train. This would give him an opportunity of seeing the working of the line; about which many and diverse opinions were held. A carriage was to come from Sheffield for the travellers. He was dressed in the high-collared, stiff coat of the period, which gave a certain character to its wearer. The hat was allied to the coat; it was high and stout, with a substantial brim. Miss Wharton wore a dark dress of linsey-woolsey, and over it a red frieze cloak lined with white silk, over that a sable boa, with cuffs and muff to match;

with a beaver hat bearing in front the three feathers of the Prince of Wales: the attire then fashionable. A very handsome, high-bred, well-dressed young lady she looked. Indeed the pair would have attracted attention in Pall Mall itself. They left shortly after daybreak; caught the coach at Sheffield at about ten o'clock; and got into Birmingham some hours after darkness had set in.

Next morning John Wharton saw his sister off safely; Lady Barbara's carriage would meet her at Watford.

He spent the day in Birmingham, and left for Sheffield next morning. He found the Chartists of Birmingham in a very restless mood; and the anticipation of rioting in the winter very strong. Already some serious outrages had been perpetrated, and people were full of apprehension. He could not help feeling very anxious about the outlook. He said to himself—'It is hunger we have to fear. If the masses could be fed there would be no riots. From the beginning there have been bread-riots; and taxed bread will lead to rioting again. Soon after the Corn Law was passed there were bread-riots; in the winter of '31-32 the Bristol bread-riots were followed by rick-burning and fire-raising; and it seems only too probable that similar riots will come in the winter, after the bad harvest.' He had heard a speaker argue strongly for a return to the old Poor Law; his child was dying at home, and might live if the necessary articles could be procured for it; but his wages, such as they were, would not allow him to provide for it what it needed; and the law would not permit of out-door relief. The case was undoubtedly a hard one. Perhaps, he thought, if we knew something more of the inner life of these rioters, we might be able to make some excuse for their wild deeds.

On the return journey the conversation ran mainly on the Chartists and their doings, or the proceedings of the Anti-Corn Law League. One passenger in the coach stated that a rumour was current in Birmingham, before he left, that Lord Brougham had been killed by a carriage accident on Penrith Beacon, a few miles from Brougham Hall. But the news was received very calmly. A few years earlier the event would have been regarded as a truly national affair. The figure of Lord Brougham,—so prominent from the time of the trial of Queen Caroline to the Reform Bill, and in some of the measures carried by the Reformed Parliament,—had recently receded very markedly. Instead of figuring before the public, and looked up to almost as much as the Monarch, or the Duke himself, he had been living in retirement in the North. Few believed the rumour.

However, the next morning, obituary notices appeared in a number of the leading London dailies, leaving no doubt about the matter.

Quickly followed a contradiction; and it seemed the old practical joker had set the rumour going to see what the press would have to say about him. Whether the results were to his mind or not, may be questioned. The effect was to set the tide of public feeling further against him. A few days later John Wharton was at Gaythorne Hall, seeing his uncle, and telling him how Edith was getting on, when he pulled out a journal.

'There is the "Spectator" uncle : there is something in it you would like to see.'

'I don't think so.'

'Well, look ! Do you see these lines about Lord Brougham ?'

'The seditious old demagogue ! After this last freak I should think people are done with him. What are they ? Oh, I see ;' and he proceeded to read them.

'WHY DID YOU DIE?'

'Oh, why did you die, Lord Brougham, Lord Brougham?
At this time of all others, Lord Brougham, Lord
    Brougham !
When but just to sustain a new part you had learned,
And you revelled in praise you once would have
    spurned ;
When time of its Terrors had Obloquy shorn,
And you grew sleek and fat on royalty's scorn :

When, too, pleasure the path of your downfall had
　　smoothed,
When enlivened by rakes, and by dowagers soothed ;
　　　　Oh ! Why did you die ?

‘ But why did you *not* die, Lord Brougham, Lord
　　Brougham,
Some five summers ago, Lord Brougham, Lord
　　Brougham ?
When your path it was straight, and your honour was
　　bright,
And the spirit of nations rejoiced in your sight ;
When each despot with fear at your eloquence shook,
And you had not been *retained* to bespatter the Duke ;
Nor for Tory applause you had bartered your fame,
Nor your country had robbed of another great name ;
　　　　Why didn’t you die ?

‘ But now choose your own time, Lord Brougham, Lord
　　Brougham ;
You may die when you please, Lord Brougham, Lord
　　Brougham !
For your life now belongs to its holder alone ;
And Lord Brougham may do what he likes with his
　　own.
Come the blow when it may, we have learned to
　　support
The sharp pang that has once been inflicted in sport ;
And the day shall by England unheeded pass by,
Nor the ready tear drop from Montgomery’s eye,
When you really do die, when you really do die.’

　　‘ Capital ! served the aged trickster
right ! There was always too much of the

actor about Brougham, to my mind. I don't think the fellow over honest.'

'Well, this cannot raise him in public estimation.'

'And yet the reforming party were simply crazy about him once. It is a lesson you can lay to heart, Jack!'

In the afternoon the Squire was talking confidentially to Mrs. Allonby, and, among other things, he said :

'It is a great trial to me to have to see my nephew and my niece both going in radical directions. Miss Edith engaged to a man who holds with the Chartists : and Mr. Jack taking up with the daughter of Mr. Carlyon —the Anti-Corn Law man. I fear it is a judgment upon me. I ought to have thrown the past behind me, and married boldly. I fear I decided wrongly.'

Why had the old Squire not married ? and what was it to which he referred ? Something evidently known to Mrs. Allonby as well as himself. A close secret clearly.

CHAPTER XII.

THE PAST WILL NOT BE BURIED.

IN the autumn of 1799, a carriage and pair might be seen standing in one of the streets which run off· English Street, in 'the border city,' waiting at a door. In it were two officers of the garrison, who had evidently lunched. They were in high spirits, a little boisterous, but not intoxicated. There was nothing about them incompatible with the social regulations of the times; when to be a trifle excited after a meal provoked no censorious comment. They were well-bred, gentlemanly young fellows; officers, a little indifferent to the opinion of civilians,—and disposed to do as they liked in some matters where probably their conduct would have been more guarded had they lived in the immediate neighbourhood of their respective families. A little indiscretion upon the part of garrison officers was not severely criticized at Carlisle, and was condoned as a part of the warrior's life; for making love when not engaged in fighting seemed then—perhaps since, certainly up to that time—the soldier's natural occupation and amusement. They did not wait to the point of impatience before they were joined by two girls; young like themselves, and also in full high spirits. Two tall, good-looking girls they were, of that light order which is found in garrison towns; possibly not unknown elsewhere. There was nothing unusual about their appearance; they were well-behaved, and even modest-looking. There was nothing of the fastness of the *demi-monde* about them; probably they were dressmakers, or seamstresses. They took their seats quietly, pretty much as a matter-of-course; as if they were quite familiar with this kind of proceeding, and betrayed no consciousness that there was anything unusual, or gravely improper, in what they were doing. It was quite clear that public opinion did not criticize such proceedings very harshly, nor was very censorious about such things,—provided a decent behaviour was maintained.

The carriage went away down the hill across the long bridge over the Eden, and breaking into a gallop the horses went at Stanwix Hill, and were half way up it before they settled down into a sober walk. It was a bright afternoon; and the sun shone clearly away over the castle with its old square tower, and embrasures,—keeping watch and ward over one great entrance to the Scottish marches. The cathedral stood out boldly; and behind it and to the west could be seen the high grounds leading up to Caldbeck Fells, and over that again the towering mass of Skiddaw; whose ' red glare waked the burghers of Carlisle,' in the days of old; and was to do it again before long—when Napoleon's design of invading

England was to rouse the island as the Armada roused it of yore. Probably the occupants of the carriage thought little of these historical associations, and of their surroundings; probably never even spoke of Kimmont Willie, and the hole in Carlisle Castle walls, where Buccleuch dug him out one stormy night; while inside they were busy erecting the gallows for him. Hard rough border fellows; but they knew something of mutual dependence, man on man; before sociology was thought of as a science. Passing the clean white houses of Stanwix, with the Scottish hills in front, Roxburgh on one side, and Dumfries on the other, they entered the long straight road which led to the Scottish border. It was the road from Carlisle to Gretna Green, then and still more after notorious for runaway matches. Once over the border the blacksmith soon made them one; before the pursuant parents,—the angry father, or guardian of the fair one, could interfere. If the historical associations of the locality

did not engage the attention of the occupants of the carriage, it is pretty certain
that the postilion's mind was reviewing the
many numerous flights and pursuits in
which he had borne a part in past days.
The sympathies of 'the road' were all
with the expectant lovers. The fast horses
were told off for the fugitives; while the
slow pairs were retained for the pursuers.
Runaway pairs for Gretna were a distinct
feature of the Bush Hotel at Carlisle in
the days of old. Tired and panting, the
horses put in at Penrith, laboured up
Botchergate, reeking with their efforts, but
well aware that their task was over. No
time was lost to speed the young folks to
Gretna, to marry in haste; too often to
repent at leisure! The postilion's features
might be seen breaking into a smile as they
passed the crest of the ridge, and he recognized a bank up which he drove the carriage
of a pursuing party; when he discerned ahead
of him an accident to the carriage of the
runaways. The old gentleman got out and

stormed, and raged, and swore wickedly
as he saw the others creeping away; while
his own vehicle was hopelessly disabled by
the accident. He accused the postilion of
complicity, and declared he would have
him indicted for conspiracy; he would sue
him; in fact, he did not know what he
would, or would not, do to him. All the
time the postilion, affecting the greatest
concern for his vehicle, kept looking it
over, surveying the situation, doing anything, indeed, to kill time; or that could
furnish an excuse for delay in attempting
to get the carriage on the road again.
He laughed aloud as he remembered how,
when they had got started again, they had
not reached the Esk before they met the
runaways,—having been irrevocably made
one, returning at a leisurely pace. There
was no longer need for haste. The paternal
anger would need time for it to blow
over: while repentance did not set in
till a much later period.

Experience had taught the hotel-keepers

that they could trust the generosity of the bridegroom in the matter of any damage to vehicles overturned, or otherwise injured, in his service.   There was no need to have from these Romeos a promise in writing to repair, or make good all damages.   They were always ready to pay all out of the fortune of the lady upon whom they had conferred the honour of wifehood.   Such were his thoughts evidently.   It was from the top of Stanwix brow that the postilion of the runaways looked back to seek for the pursuers; if they were not on Eden bridge, they would not arrive at Gretna till the ceremony was concluded.

These runaway marriages led to some further irregularities.   To be married at Gretna grew to be not uncommonly a sort of freak,—never seriously intended as marriage by either of the contracting parties. Persons whose relations were rather those of 'spiritual husbands and wives' than those of 'lawful husbands and wives,' not unfrequently went through a ceremony over the border,—which was held at least as some extenuation of their unsanctified union.

Such alliances not rarely ended in mutual desire for separation; while the parties each contracted new and lasting ties. Nor was any divorce, or formal arrangement, required in the dissolving of these fleeting ties. If the parties were mutually satisfied; then an ordinary marriage succeeded the irregular one, and all was well. But if the association was found to become distasteful in time, the whilom man and wife each went their own way, unmolested by the other. Many of the border-marriages were never meant to be lasting. It was never understood that either party should look upon the affair in a serious light.

Consequently, when the carriage had driven over the Esk, and was nearing the little rivulet which forms the actual boundary-line betwixt England and Scotland, the idea was started of undergoing a mock-union at Gretna; and the proposal met with ready acceptance. Many an officer at Carlisle Castle had undergone a Scottish marriage in this thoughtless manner; nor had any practical inconvenience been experienced afterwards in consequence thereof. When the officer went with his regiment elsewhere, the nymph sought another lord; and never thought of troubling him in any way, or interfering with any ties he might subsequently contract. The marriage-tie has different associations in the northern kingdom than in its southern neighbour; and the relations of the sexes were somewhat mixed along the border.

The girls were delighted at the proposition; and turning their rings with the plain portion to the back of the hand, the requisite golden circle was readily improvisoed. It would be a capital lark. As the gentle ascent from the little Sark was made, the practical joke was decided upon. When they drove up to the little inn the landlord met them.

'Ye've brocht a fine day with ye the

day, captain!' he remarked. (No officer
was ever of lower rank than 'Captain,'
when out on a merry-making expedition.)
'And my leddy, too, I see. Gude afternoon, leddies,' he continued.

'You are a little premature, Sandy. We
shall require the services of your neighbour
before the ladies can claim us. I dare say
he will not keep us waiting long,' said one.

'Marry, will he not. He'll fasten ye in
less time than he can turn a horse-shoe.
Ye'll sune be back married folks. Forsooth,
will ye put up the horses?—they'll no' object
to a rest.'

'Yes; you may as well take out the
horses,' replied the officers. 'We will stay
an hour or two, and drive back in the
moonlight. It is the harvest-moon, Sandy,
eh?'

'Weel, yes; it luiks rayther a moonlight
job athegither, to my mind,' was the canny
response. 'Maun I whustle "Haste to the
wedding" for ye? Though whustling's
no' much of a practeece o' mine. You'll

win throo' the job wi'out music, I'll warrant ye,' he went on. People contracting
irregular marriages are not likely to
resent some familiarity from a complaisant
Boniface.

So they turned away to the blacksmith's
shop at the end of the inn ; so well known,
and so well remembered, by many a couple.
The blacksmith's shop stood at the northern
end of the inn ; and forms now the drawing-room of a handsome country house.
The smith, Andrew Jardine, was in no way
surprised at two couples presenting themselves at his shop as the altar of Hymen,
where he officiated as high priest. He
thought he had seldom seen two better-
looking couples together before in the whole
of his long experience.

'Whilk maun I mary first ?' he inquired.

A fair-haired man with a dark girl came
forward.

'Just gie me your names, please ?'

'Edward Wharton' ; and 'Lilian Anderson' were the respective answers.

'Ye tek this woman to be your wedded wife?'

'Certainly, I do,' said the officer.

'And ye tek this maun for your wedded husband; do ye, my wench?'

'I do,' was the reply; the girl being abashed by the rude address of the officiating priest; who readily detected that the whole was a freak, and that nothing serious was contemplated.

'Then I pronounce ye one!' he answered. 'You'll hae your marriage-lines, of coorse?' Not well seeing how to refuse the document, the girl waited until the old smith had written a few lines; a certificate of the marriage, in fact.

It was more to get rid of the thing than anything else, that the bride put the slip of dingy paper into her purse. As to the bridegroom, he looked upon the matter as a useless formality. He liked the girl, was fond of her: but as to his wife, he would as soon have dreamt of marrying one of the post-horses. He was a patrician, and would only marry in his own order.

The other couple were soon disposed of; and Andrew took a fee which made him sorry that he had made so free with one of the girls. He, however, refrained from giving them his blessing; a part of the ceremony he never omitted when the matter 'lookit business,' as he called it.

'They're braw young folks,' was his comment. 'I wonder hoo soon they'll forgit auld Andrew Jardine, and Gretna?'

Returning to the inn they had some claret; Sandie pronouncing, with a keen eye to his own interests, that nothing else was good enough for such an occasion.

'Whuskey's well eneugh for th' ordinar' couples. But for the likes of you, gentlemen, naithing but claret's becomin'. Ye've no' a day like this ivvery day,' he persisted; affecting to regard the affair as serious, and the ceremony as valid.

The girls enjoyed the fun; the respective couples behaved and spoke to each other as

if the marriage was a reality; and laughed
at the strange sound of the 'Mrs.'; and
thought it was a good joke. In fact, there
was merely the folly and frolic of the
optimism of youth. Little did any one of
the four think then that the echo of that
laughter would be distinctly heard in the
far-away years of the distant future.

In the falling evening, after the sun had
set behind Criffel Fell, the horses were put
to again, and the party drove back to
Carlisle; every one feeling that they had
had a pleasant excursion. Nor did these
brides remind their lords of the wedding
ceremony except in joke. When Lilian
Anderson was designated 'Mrs. Wharton,'
sometimes she was pleased, at other times
cross, according to her mood. In a little
time the incident seemed to have slipped
out of the memory of all concerned in it;
as much from the parties who formed the
chief actors, as the high priest who officiated; unless it was when Lilian encountered the little slip of paper, her marriage-

lines, in the recesses of her little box of treasures.

Lilian's father was a shepherd in the Bewcastle Fells; more 'having' and less scrupulous than their neighbours, the Bewcastle people, were said to be. Such was their reputation; and when, by an accident, the canny shepherd heard of the mock-wedding, he had no hesitation in setting to see what could be made of it. So he put himself into communication with young Wharton, who then became aware that he had committed a very foolish act. In vain the girl tried her best to persuade her father to abandon his purpose, for she knew Lieutenant Wharton was not the man to make any terms with him: he would not be dissuaded. So the young lieutenant applied for leave of absence, procured it; then said good-bye to Lilian and 'the merrie city;' and before long news reached the garrison, and from thence spread outwards, that Lieutenant Wharton had exchanged into a regiment going out to Canada. The Bewcastle man chafed; he had taken nothing by his persistence except to place an ugly obstacle in the way of his daughter being properly married, by attaching importance to old Andrew Jardine's marriage certificate. Lilian fretted, and became very unhappy; probably in this result, the obstacle to her being legally married some day was the smallest factor.

It was a few years after Mr. Charles Wharton, the eldest brother of the family, had come to the estates, that a tall woman of the working-class, of respectable appearance, though her clothes were stained with travel, knocked at the servants' entrance of Gaythorne Hall. Mrs. Allonby was then parlour-maid, and happening to be in the way when the knock was heard, answered the door.

'Is this Squire Wharton's?' the stranger asked.

After an affirmative answer, she inquired:

'Is Lieutenant Edward at home?'

The tones were rather faltering. Mary

Allonby was a quick-witted girl, with a full
share of feminine curiosity in her composition.
She knew there was a drop of wild blood in
the Whartons, and the Lieutenant was said
to share in the inheritance. A good-looking
woman of the lower orders asking for him
roused her suspicions.

'Come in this way,' she said, showing the
traveller into a room rarely used. 'Where
do you come from?'

'I come fra Carlisle,' was the response.
'I knew the Lieutenant when he was at the
Castle there. I've been unfortunate; and
I ken the Lieutenant would help me if he
knew; for the days of auld lang syne.'

Mary Allonby recognized the accent;
for her father came from the north, and
retained much of his northern twang. She
got the visitor some food, and gained her
confidence. Before long she was in possession of the whole story; and saw for herself
the bit of faded paper which Lilian regarded
rather as a voucher for the accuracy of her
story, than as giving her any claim upon

the Lieutenant. She preferred no legal claim ; she came simply as a suitor, hoping help from his generosity.

Mary knew well enough that the Lieutenant would have listened to the tale had he been at home, and befriended the woman ; though if any positive claim had been made upon him he would have fiercely resented it.

When the stranger learned that he was still in Canada, she became greatly distressed and disturbed. What little money she had, had been expended on the way ; and she had hoped to have heard that the Lieutenant was in England, where a letter would find him in a few days. She had no voucher of character to enable her to get work ; even if she would have cared to remain in the neighbourhood of Gaythorne Hall, where her connection with the Lieutenant would be sure to get out.

This turn of the conversation showed Mary that the woman's story was a true one. She had no design to extort money

from the family, and evidently wanted her
errand to be kept a secret. Mary took a
resolve,—partly the outcome of good feeling,
partly from self-interest. The Squire would
never live to be an old man like his father;
his life was not compatible with old age:
he was a bachelor, and likely to remain
one; the Lieutenant would some day be
Squire. It was worth the risk.

So she took two pounds out of her
savings, and gave them to her visitor so
that she might make her way back to
Carlisle. The gratitude of the woman was
boundless.

Mary showed her out without being seen.
No one would be likely to ask questions;
and the traveller was not likely to answer
them, if they did. The secret was safe.

How could she let the Lieutenant know?
She dared not write a letter. The post-
office at Brigstone would soon detect the
letter; and surmises would be conjectured
of anything but a pleasing character.

There was no hurry. At last she saw

her way. Squire Charles was a careless personage, and a bad correspondent. He disliked the bother of writing letters, and sealing them up. All the house knew when he was going to write a letter to the Lieutenant.

Mary bided her time. One day he announced his intention of writing a letter. She got the butler out of the way. When the sealing came there was no wax: the Squire would not wait, so he rang the bell, and told Mary to seal the letter for him. She knew well enough why the sealing-wax was not at hand; and when the letter was dispatched, her own little missive lay safe inside it.

When the Lieutenant received his brother's letter, he found within a slip, on which was written :

'HONOURED SIR,

'Lilian Anderson was here the other day. She was in want of money, so I gave her two pounds. Hoping you are well, as this leaves us all here,

'I am, yours respectfully,

'MARY ALLONBY.'

He was thunderstruck. The girl had been at Gaythorne Hall asking for him : and in want too ! The letter was terribly meagre, he felt. What was her object? As was natural, his apprehensions suggested the worst. Mary had advanced her two pounds out of her own money. There must have been some strong reason for her to do that : for she would know that he could not send it to her without exciting suspicion, and setting inquiries on foot. He could not write to her for further particulars. He felt in a maze of doubt, from which he could not extricate himself. There must, too, have been some strong pressure on Lilian to have carried her to Gaythorne Hall.

He felt wretched about it. It was clear that freak at Gretna was to hang like a millstone round his neck for the rest of his life. He could not well institute inquiries at Carlisle ; that would be as good as acknowledging there was something in the marriage. He cursed the thoughtlessness

which prompted the foolish freak. Many
a time as he was on the banks of the
Saguenay river, along the shores of the
great lakes, in the solitude of a Canadian
forest, the remembrance of that luckless
afternoon,—that journey across the Scotch
border, rose up before him. The bitterness
of the memory waxed as time wore on ; and
his imagination wove a whole network of
conjectures around the visit to Gaythorne
Hall. Had he something tangible to deal
with, he felt it would be less irksome.
Had some definite action been taken ; had
Lilian asserted that she was his wife, then
he could take positive action. All he knew
was that she was in poverty ; and had gone
all the way into South Yorkshire to inquire
after him ; that Mary Allonby had advanced
two pounds on his account. What had
made the girl do that ? He could not
write !

The thing became the *bête noir* of his
existence. He welcomed the war which
broke out ; amidst the cares, the occupation

of active warfare, he felt a distraction from these absorbing thoughts. He was naturally courageous; his private trouble made him even reckless. And Lieutenant Wharton was conspicuous for fearlessness where all were brave.

At last his brother's death made it necessary to return to England; and, with the hearty good wishes of his comrades, Captain Wharton set out for England, to doff his uniform and take his position as an English Squire. He found Mary Allonby occupying the place of housekeeper: a post which the death of the old occupant of the position had made vacant; and Squire Charles hated new faces. As soon as convenient he asked the particulars of Lilian's visit: he was told all. It was clear there was no claim preferred; but it was not equally clear that some claim might not be preferred now that he was at home, and the owner of the Wharton property. The garrison at Carlisle, though not the regiment in which he served there, would furnish a means of gaining information about him, if any one was determined to know. Lilian, like himself, must be approaching middle age; she must be five-and-thirty. What was she doing? He would willingly make provision for her. It was evident that her visit to Gaythorne Hall had no sinister intent. She did not mean to harass, or annoy him: that was obvious. What was it, then? His doubts and anxieties were scarcely lessened. Was Lilian still single? That he could not ascertain without raising awkward suggestions, and a certain amount of admission that she had a claim upon him.

Squire Wharton, as he was now termed, found, like many another man, that the tie —lightly and thoughtlessly contracted, when held as no tie, might grow to be a fetter as years roll on. He had been a warrior, and knew well:

'The sound of a kiss is not so loud as that of a cannon, but its echo lasts a deal longer.'

So it does!

Consequently he remained single. Unmarried, he was safe from anything more than mere annoyance; but if he married, the aspect of matters was profoundly altered. He would be liable to be worried beyond endurance. Even a charge of bigamy might possibly be preferred against him. The Squire shrank from the prospect; and abjured all thought of matrimony.

Mrs. Allonby, however, had made her place secure during the natural lifetime of the Squire and herself. She had made a good investment of her two pounds. Besides, she held the Squire's secret!

END OF VOL. II.